# UNCONTROLLED

THE POWER SERIES: BOOK FOUR

## VICTORIA WOODS

UNCONTROLLED

First Edition. August 31, 2021.

Copyright© 2021 by Victoria Woods

ISBN: 978-1-7361258-8-5

# TABLE OF CONTENTS

For all the women with dreams that may seem too big to achieve...

Just start. You can do this.

Regret is a bigger b*tch than fear.

TRIGGER WARNING

*Subject matters like rape, abuse, and human trafficking that may be dark and disturbing to some readers is included in this book. None of these topics are glorified or deemed as acceptable in this book.*

# CHAPTER I

## CLAIRE

*Present Day*

*Semya*. Family.

Painted in dull orange angular font over the massive wood doors, the word chided me through the car window. I imagined my brother's thick voice lecturing me on the importance of family and how I had shamed the Petrov name by running away.

He had given Maman and I no choice when he plotted against Papa. Although Leonid was not my mother's biological child, we shared a bloodline through our father. Leonid's mother, a native Russian, was Papa's first wife. They had only had one child together, a son, to carry on the Petrov name and rule over the Bratva in the event of Papa's death, provided none

1

of the other Brothers objected. They rarely did unless the new ruler was deemed unfit, either due to waning health or deceit against the Brothers. They were loyal to no one but themselves. If one of their own were found to be dishonest to another, they would be killed in the most heinous of ways.

This stipulation extended to family members of the Bratva, too. It was the reason Leonid's mother had been murdered at the command of my father, Nicholai Petrov. When it was discovered that she had been having a secret affair with one of Papa's guards right under his roof, her fate was sealed. Leonid was barely a teenager when our father had her hanged in the back yard of the family estate with the Brothers and Leonid in attendance to remind everyone that disloyalty would never be tolerated. The guard was later disemboweled in front of the same audience to further drive the lesson home.

Father was left wifeless, and Leonid, not more than fourteen years old, was left marred with a wound that would never heal. Instead, it only festered, sending poisonous vengeance coursing through his veins.

Before the final handful of dirt had been thrown atop Leonid's mother's unmarked grave, Papa had found himself a new wife, Camille.

Maman said she was born and raised in the south of France, but that was all she'd ever shared. I didn't even know her maiden name. She had never spoken much of her life before marrying my father. As a matter of fact, I didn't know anything about her family or how she had even met Papa in the first place. It was evident that they hadn't married for love because I couldn't remember him ever showing her affection.

Papa had rarely ever shown me love either. He had been very stern and had kept me locked in the house for most of my childhood. Even tutors would come to the estate for my formal education, so I didn't have to leave for school.

Our home spanned acres of land and was heavily secured with guards like a fortress—or a prison, depending on the point of view of the person describing it. Because of the isolation we were forced to endure, Maman and I shared a bond stronger than most mothers and daughters had. We both experienced the same distress, except for me, it wasn't something I had chosen. I was born into it.

After Leonid killed Papa, he returned to the estate as the new *Pakhan,* since he was the rightful heir to the throne. The first and only son of the fallen leader. Unbeknownst to the Brothers, his hands were stained with his own father's blood. All but one welcomed him as their leader and pledged fidelity to him.

Mikhail was one of the oldest members of the brotherhood, having been there before my father took the throne. He was the one who had protected us during our time in Russia and informed Maman of her stepson's crimes. In the cover of night, Mikhail helped us escape before Leonid could find us—or rather, me. He provided us with new identities, removing any trace of Karina Petrov from the world. My new name was Claire Varon, and Maman went by Sylvie Varon.

We moved quickly in the night. Luckily, we were able to slip past the guards with Mikhail's help. He hid us in the back of his SUV and drove out of the compound without tipping off any of the guards. Because he was the senior-most member, he had earned a level of respect. The younger men knew not to question him. All except Leonid.

After traveling for hours, we arrived at a loading dock outside of what seemed like a factory. Silently, we slipped into the back of a truck filled with cargo consisting of some sort of grain—maybe milled wheat. I could still remember the overwhelmingly sweet and nutty smell and the way the tiny grain-like particles tickled my nose as the burlap bags shifted, kicking up dust, during our journey.

The driver had apparently had a deal with Mikhail because they shook hands before we pulled away from the dock. The truck rolled and bounced us for days, only stopping for brief periods of time when the driver would knock on the back of the gate before tossing in wrapped packages of warm bread and cured meat, which Maman and I ate hungrily. We shared a canteen of water between the two of us, and the driver would only let us out in desolate areas to relieve ourselves. He never spoke to us, barely acknowledging our presence. I often wondered if it was safe to even trust him.

What if he had been planning to sell us like my father had often done to women and children? I knew about Papa's trafficking business but had never asked questions. What little I did know already kept me up at night. How would I ever sleep again once I had answers to the questions that swirled in my head?

We traveled for ages. The only thing that helped us pass the time was imagining the new life that awaited us in France. I had never been out of Russia and had barely been beyond the walls of our estate.

Maman painted a vivid picture of Paris for me. She told me what she could remember of it when she visited as a child. I could hear the chatter of pedestrians bustling around the city. I could smell the perfume of the flower stands. I could taste the buttery flavor of a flakey croissant. The worry that had filled my gut when we left the compound was replaced with a new feeling—hope. Hope that Maman and I would soon get the life that we deserved...

Now, I no longer held any hope that I would ever find myself out of this life. I had run away from it once, and here I was, plunged right back into it.

I sat in the Uber in front of the restaurant, praying that I would soon wake up from the nightmare that had been revived the second my brother texted me. He must have known I would come without the use of force. I didn't have a choice. I should have known after Maman's death that Leonid could find me anywhere.

How I made my way out of the car and to the front door of the restaurant was a blur. The pounding of my heartbeat in my ears drowned out the sounds of the street. My only focus was on steadying my shaking knees.

The polished door handle felt smooth underneath my hand. The heaviness of the door silently queried me; did I really want to enter? *No.* But if I didn't go to him, he'd come for me.

The small chamber housing the empty hostess stand reminded me of my home in Kazan. The dim lighting coupled with the red and gold décor was very old-school Russian, and very much reminiscent of my father's style—traditional and harsh.

Judging from the lack of restaurant staff, it was safe to assume that Leonid had shut the restaurant down for the day. The fewer witnesses around, the better.

I pushed aside the heavy velvet curtain that blocked the rest of the restaurant from view and stepped through.

"There she is!" I heard Leonid's voice before I had even fully entered the room. He must have been waiting for me, ready to punish me for disobeying the family code.

The years that had passed hadn't aged him much since I last saw him. He still sported the same sandy blond, shortly shaved hairstyle. His short height and green eyes weren't inherited from our father, who had brown eyes, but had most likely come from his mother. I had never seen photos of her since Papa had removed them all, and the staff had been forbidden from ever mentioning her.

His face seemed more hardened if anything, but his smile still never quite met his eyes, just like I remembered.

"It has been far too long, sister. Come. We have a lot of catching up to do." He motioned to the chair in front of the table.

My cowering brain submitted to old habits and my body followed his orders. The years of fending for myself hadn't done much to stiffen my spine when faced by one of the two tyrants of my childhood.

The other face from my past was already seated at the table, my cousin Igor. I winced as his toothless grin was replaced by a swipe of his tongue over his bottom lip, as if he were ready to devour me. My stomach roiled at his presence, the same as it always had when I was around him as a child.

The son of Papa's sister, Igor was our half cousin and since he was only a few years younger than Leonid, the two had been attached at the hip when they were growing up.

7

Being my relative and at least ten years my senior had never stopped him from casting lecherous glances at me when we were younger. His glare had only grown more lustful and disturbing now that I was an adult.

I focused my eyes on Leonid instead, trying to wall out the ravenous ogre next to him. "What do you want, Leonid?" By the grace of some higher power, my voice remained trained and steady.

"Ah, straight to the point. No time to chat first? You've been away for over five years. A lot must have happened in that time." He leaned in closer, the glint of evil in his eyes sharp enough to pierce my skin from across the table.

I leaned back in my chair to avoid the pain of the slice he was withholding; I knew he was just waiting for the right moment to attack.

"You were obviously looking for me. And you found me, so cut the shit."

"Oh! Such a filthy mouth! So much change in all this time? New city. New hair. New name! I barely recognize you anymore, *Karina*."

I cringed at the mention of my birth name. *Karina.* The name that my father had chosen for me when I was born.

I nervously fingered a lock of my bottle blonde hair. My mother and I had both been born with the same honey-brown hair color but had dyed it blonde to change our appearance. Maman had gone a step further and used colored contacts to hide her blue eyes but never insisted I change mine, probably because I was too young to fiddle with contact lenses at the time.

"My apologies. I hear you go by Claire now. What a beautiful name your mother chose for you."

So, he didn't know that it was Mikhail who had secured our new identities...

"By the way, where is she now?" he mocked me, pretending to look around the restaurant for her.

"Fuck you," I spat reflexively. He knew perfectly well that she was six feet under. He'd fucking put her there.

In a flash, Igor launched out of his seat, his hands ready to throttle my neck over the table. I jumped back, sending my chair tumbling over behind me. Leonid's grip stopped Igor, and subsequently shoved him back into his seat, sending the table shaking as his knees knocked the underside of it.

"I know it was you. I know what you did to Maman," I seethed. He thought I was an idiot, but I knew he was the one who'd killed my mother, even if the police could never prove it. I leaned in closer to him, eyeing the line of guards standing at attention at the back of the restaurant, out of earshot. Lowering my voice, emulating the deathly tone my father used on my mother all those years ago, I said, "And if you don't let me walk out of here, I'll tell your Brothers who else's blood you have on your hands."

"You have no proof," he ground out between tightly clenched teeth. Leonid's nostrils flared, producing an audible grunt like that of a cornered animal.

Igor's throat bobbed with a nervous swallow—his own guilt obvious. Of course, he would have been involved.

"Careful, brother. You're starting to show through your cracks." I grinned, satisfied that I had affected both in such a way.

If the Brothers only knew that he had killed their former *Pakhan*, he would be as good as dead. I never had the chance to oust him since I was running for my life and couldn't risk it if the rest of the Bratva didn't believe me. I was sure Mikhail never revealed the truth since he didn't want anyone finding out that he helped Maman and me escape.

"Enough!" he roared, spittle flying in every direction. His ears reddened with rage. "Sit the fuck down, you whore."

I bent over to right my chair. His rage seemed to be wholly from our father. Hate ran through their veins stronger than blood.

My butt found the seat to avoid further tempting my brother to put a bullet between my eyes. He should have by now, and the fact that I was still alive meant that he wanted something.

One of his men approached the table and set plates of food in front of us. My appetite was dead to the familiar mixed aroma of cold sausage soup and braised beets.

Igor didn't wait for either of us to start eating before he stuffed his mouth. Rivulets of broth streamed down his chin.

"Eat," Leonid instructed. "We have important business to discuss."

"Like what?" What business could I have with the Bratva? I was no one anymore. The estranged stepsister to the *Pakhan* was hardly a role of importance.

"Your new boyfriend."

My heart stilled. *Jai.* When Leonid texted me about wanting to meet my boyfriend, I'd panicked. Jai was innocent in all of this, and because of my fucked-up past, I had pinned a flaming target to his back.

We had finally reached a place where we could truly open up to each other. I had wanted so badly to share my ghosts with him tonight, and now here they were, risen from the grave and sitting right in front of me.

My main goal right now was to appease my brother and make it out of here alive to be able to tell Jai to run for his life. Maybe he could hide out somewhere for a bit until Leonid was off his back. His family had money, and I was hoping it would be enough to get out of the mess I had dragged him into. I loved him so much

11

that I couldn't bear the thought of him leaving, but if it meant he would be safe, then I would have to let him go.

"I don't know what you're talking about," I replied after too long of a pause, crossing my arms over my chest to close myself off to him.

"Don't play stupid with me. It's an ugly look on you. I know you are a smart girl...too smart, sometimes." He paused, as if reconsidering his train of thought. "Yet, when it comes to him, I suppose you are rather stupid." He rubbed a finger lazily along his fat lip and smirked. "I guess, *love* is blinding."

"You know nothing about him," I shouted in defense.

He let out a shrill laugh. Switching to Russian, he scoffed and said, "*I know nothing about him? Sweetheart, you really have no clue who you're dating.*"

I furrowed my brow, completely puzzled. I had no doubt that he had a complete file of research on him by now from the cocky way he spoke. Jai had never been an open book, but like me, he'd finally seemed ready to share his secrets. However, I was certain that there was no way his demons were scarier than mine.

Something caught Leonid's attention over my shoulder, and his mouth fixed into a devious grin. My gut screamed at me not to turn around. Instead, I sat ramrod straight in my chair as heavy footsteps approached. The slapping of soles on the hardwood behind me sent the hairs on the back of my neck standing on

12

end. One pair of shoes? No. Two. Expensive shoes. The type that only bad men could afford. Bad men like Leonid.

Were these men here to kidnap me? Or do something worse?

Leonid stood up, eager to greet his guests. "Welcome, boys! So nice of you to join us! Come join us for lunch." He motioned to the two vacant seats flanking the table.

The footsteps grew closer. I could feel my eardrums vibrating with the intensity of each step. If I threw up on the table in front of me, would that be enough to send these villains running? Maybe Leonid would be so disgusted with my weakness that he'd just leave me be to live out the rest of my days quietly here in New York. I would agree to move off the grid if it meant that I would never have to feel this anxiety again.

"You seem to have caught us right on time. Say hello to my friends, sister." The clunking against the wood floor ceased.

Not many people even knew I existed since I wasn't another son, as Nicholai had so desperately wanted. Whoever was behind me was just as wicked as my brother. Leonid was no doubt thrilled at catching them off guard with my presence.

I didn't move to greet these monsters. My fear was strong enough, keeping my ass glued to my seat.

"Get up, girl." Leonid's eyes flamed with menace and his hands clenched into fists on the tabletop, primed and ready to make contact with my jaw. My hesitance had read as disobedience,

13

and he wasn't about to let it compromise his aura of power and dominance in front of company.

I rose slowly from my seat, my brain screaming for me to run out the back entrance and never look back. Turning around to face yet more villains than were already in front of me, I clenched my fists so tightly at my sides that my nails sliced into my palms. The self-inflicted sting was one last desperate attempt to wake myself up from this nightmare.

My eyes fixated on a chocolate pair staring back at me, mirroring my shock. I had stared into them in the throes of bliss and watched them squint in laughter when their owner was at his happiest, but never had I seen them this wide with horror.

"Jai," I uttered in disbelief. My mind raced to come up with an explanation I could stomach to why he would be here with Zayn by his side, a desperate attempt to distract myself from the most obvious reason.

Leonid's loud chuckle emanated from behind me as he addressed Jai. "I believe you've met. Jai Sethi, this is my little sister, Karina Petrov. I believe you might know her as Claire Varon."

Zayn flashed Jai a side glance, uncertain. But Jai's eyes stayed on me. They darted from my hair to my face, then to my hands, like a chess player assessing the board after his opponent made a move. *Check mate.*

14

Leonid walked around the table and placed a hand on my shoulder. My body jumped at the contact, and my line of vision broke from Jai's hold, nervously fixating on my brother. His palm molded to the contour of my bone and squeezed tightly, keeping me from pulling away. I grimaced from the pressure of his stubby fingers pinching between the joint that held my shoulder blade and my arm, like he was just waiting for me to make one wrong move so he could dislocate the whole thing.

I turned my head back in time to catch Jai clench his jaw as he focused on Leonid's grip. His shoulders tensed before Zayn placed his hand on his back.

"Hmmm. I'd have imagined at least a hello between lovers. Maybe a peck on the cheek?" He looked between the two of us to see who would move first, probably so he could have an excuse to fire his weapons. "No?" He shrugged. "Suit yourselves."

I had so many questions, but I didn't dare speak unless I wanted to find myself at the receiving end of the barrel of a gun.

"Why are you here, Leonid?" Zayn spoke up.

"Why are *you* here? You're the ones who showed up here to interrupt our family reunion." Leonid let go of me and slid his hands into his pockets. "Were you hoping to ambush me again, since your last attempt on my life failed so miserably?"

Igor snorted, but Leonid didn't bother turning back to acknowledge him. Neither did I. I was too hung up on what I had just heard.

Apparently, Jai knew enough of Leonid to try to kill him. The enemies of the Bratva wanted to see them dead. Jai was clearly their enemy and probably even more heinous than Leonid.

I had been in bed with the devil.

I crossed my arms over my belly to stop the churning inside. If I didn't get a hold of myself, I'd surely puke.

Had he just been using me to get to Leonid to try to kill him again? Everything that had happened between us had been a lie. I was so stupid. Years of being the child of the Bratva should have made me smarter than this. Instead, I fell head over heels for the first handsome stranger who showed me the least bit of attention, like a fool. The betrayal tasted bitter on my tongue.

I blinked quickly to fight back the tears threatening to fall. Why the fuck wasn't Jai saying anything? I wanted him to tell me that he wasn't a terrible man like my brother and that I wasn't a toy he was using for his benefit. But as time stretched without him uttering a word, I realized that my wishes wouldn't become reality. I was just a stupid girl. Just like Maman was a stupid girl who married Papa.

"Since I ruined your assassination mission today, maybe you should join us for lunch? I was just about to discuss an important matter with my sister."

Jai and Zayn stood cemented to the ground as their pupils bounced between the two of us.

"I know this might come to you as a disappointment, Jai, but my sister has certain duties she needs to fulfill as a Petrov." Leonid's menacing grin gave away nothing as he paused to savor the tension he had so maniacally crafted in the room.

"Speak, asshole," Jai commanded suddenly, his voice surging across the empty restaurant. The anger it held made me jump.

It was the first time he had said anything since arriving, and barely a full sentence. The vein in his neck twitched visibly with impatience.

"You see, Karina...or Claire...has been raised to carry on her Bratva lineage from the time she was born. As the daughter of a former *Pakhan* and sister to the current one, her role is to strengthen our organization."

I hung on his every word, waiting to hear what foul scheme he was planning to spew.

"Now, when I heard that she had taken an interest in a Sethi brother, I had to fly here to see it for myself."

Wrapping his arm around me, he pulled me closer to his body. I could smell his rank breath and feel his sweat through my clothes. His fingers dug into my upper arm, surely leaving marks. A faint whimper escaped my lips.

My breathing picked up, yet I couldn't get enough air into my lungs. Claustrophobia constricted me from being held so tightly.

Jai must have sensed my distress because his body tensed like a beast ready to pounce. But before he could launch forward, Zayn caught his arm, holding him back.

"I'm afraid I can't allow Karina to continue her relationship with you, Jai. Her role as the daughter of the Bratva permits me to use her to her fullest potential. A bargaining chip to create new...stronger...alliances to benefit the Brotherhood."

I struggled to break free of his grasp, but he only held on to me tighter, my arm going numb from the pressure he inflicted.

"Despite what my dearest sister has tricked you into believing, she is at my disposal to marry her off to whomever I deem fit."

I whipped my head to the side towards Leonid, sheer confusion radiating off me. What the fuck was he talking about?

"Jai," I pled desperately, flashing my gaze back to him, to meet eyes full only of revulsion. I shook my head frantically, hoping he'd believe I had known nothing of this. I needed him to know that I played no part in this willingly.

"Yes, sister. I am here to bring you home to find a husband. Together, we will create a dynasty that spans countries." Leonid planted his fat, wet lips against my cheek, giving me a kiss as if we were a loving family.

# CHAPTER II

## JAI

*ind a husband?* I nearly stumbled backward from shock. It took every fiber of control in me to keep the fury storming inside from detonating. The only thing that helped me keep my shit together was the comforting warmth of my brother next to me.

She had lied to me. I was so stupid to have believed anything that had come out of her mouth. All the "I love you's" and sweet nothings she'd uttered had been bullshit. Even hearing her say my name made me want to slam my fist into a table. At least she knew my real name, which was more than I could say for her. *Karina.*

Was this the universe's fucked-up form of retribution for my sins? *Message received.*

19

I searched her eyes for any hint of the Claire that I thought I knew, but instead, all I found was poorly feigned fear and shock. This must have been what Karina was like. *A liar.* She'd have to be a good-ass one if she were the sister to the Bratva. Even her fake confusion over why I was here was believable. But I knew better now. She knew I'd come if I knew Leonid would be in town, even if she never told me about her meeting herself. Maybe Mikhail was in on this too since he was the one who informed me that his *Pakhan* would be here. I was no longer sure who I could trust.

Anything surrounding Leonid was just smoke and mirrors— mirrors I wanted to smash to a million pieces, just like whatever Claire and I had between us.

Leonid's hold on her was tight, and I could tell it was too uncomfortable for her liking, and mine. But I struggled hard to reign in any remaining sympathy I still had for her. This was what happened when you were loyal to trash like him.

I found it difficult to suppress my gut instinct to wrap my fingers around his throat. He was a sick motherfucker, and his treatment of his sister proved it. *God—sister!* Of all the women in the world, Leonid's sister had to be the one that I fell for.

He pressed a sloppy kiss to her cheek. It wasn't the kind of quick peck a sibling gave another. This was a marking of ownership. He was a dog pissing over a patch of grass to force me to heel. His lips lingered for far too long, eliciting an audible shudder from her. She had said her father had never violated her, but I couldn't be sure that Leonid hadn't touched her. He was as vile as they came, and I wouldn't have put it past him to hurt his own sister in that way.

Without thinking, I grabbed the gun that had been concealed inside of my jacket and aimed it sideways with my finger on the trigger. Instantaneously, the line of guards drew their weapons to attention, each aiming right between my eyes. Igor had pulled his weapon out too and now moved in closer to his cousin as added backup.

My men weren't inside of the restaurant, but I knew they had the building surrounded, just waiting to blow the whole place up.

I couldn't see him next to me, but I felt that Zayn was ready too. Tension radiated off his body, and I felt its fog swarm around me. He was just as lethal as I was when he was pissed. And right now, he was pissed.

"Let her go." The coolness of the metal of my weapon did little to temper my rage.

His hyena-like cackle rang in my ears. "After all that she did to you, you still want her?" He yanked her hair at the back of her head, causing her to cry out. "Her pussy must be magic. Doesn't surprise me, though. Her mother's was tight like a

21

python's squeeze on our father's dick, or so he claimed. Maybe I should have Igor take it out for a test drive and report back about his experience?"

That earned an eager snicker from his bitch boy.

Suddenly, glass shattered behind us as gunshots rang out in chorus. My boys were ready for blood.

I dodged out of their line of fire, rolling on the ground to keep myself low. With my finger still on the trigger, I took cover under a table and fired off shot after shot, taking down three of the guards.

Leonid tossed his sister over to Igor to free up his hands, then began firing his weapon wildly, releasing bullets in every direction.

My boys stormed the place with artillery in droves, clouding the room with flying shards of glass and dry wall in their wake.

Zayn was straddling one of Leonid's goons, slinging punches to his face. Blood coated his knuckles, but he heeded that no attention. He was a machine in combat.

A loud shriek sounded from Claire, or rather Karina, causing my stomach to drop. I spotted her through the smoke and bullets, struggling against Igor. His grubby hands were around her, dragging her protesting body toward the back entrance. She clawed at his arm, trying to break free, but Igor was bigger than she was, and her fighting was futile. She didn't let up, though, kicking her legs into the air to make his job harder, even though his gun was stationary at her temple. She was a fighter. That, I was still sure of.

Tired of the strain, Igor smashed the butt of his gun into the side of her face. Stunned, she stared at me in a daze, not making a sound, as if I were the only thing she could focus on before her eyes crossed and her eyelids drooped shut.

"Zayn!" I shouted to get his attention before I pushed off the ground to run to her. Closer to her than I was, Zayn issued a final blow to his assailant then took off running toward her and Igor.

A guard rushed me, launching his fist into my jaw, and knocking me onto my ass. The searing pain made my eyes tear up. He cocked his fist back again, but before he could get in another hit, a huge explosion boomed, clouding the room with thick smoke.

# CHAPTER III

## CLAIRE

I t was all a blur. The gunshots ricocheting. The fists flying. The explosion before my brain succumbed to unconsciousness.

Warmth spread from the side of my body, making me feel secure even before opening my eyes. The stillness surrounding me and the gentle rock of my body against something firm coaxed me to blink my eyes open. Everything appeared fuzzy. A few blinks more and the black leather interior of an SUV came into focus. *Where are they taking me?*

My head had been resting heavily on the strong form beside me. The clean and familiar scent of leaves sprinkled with raindrops enveloped me. Although it wasn't the spicy, dominating scent that I longed for, I still welcomed the comfort.

*Zayn.* I hadn't interacted with him much in the past, but there was something about him that I trusted. His emotions were always clearly written on his face, a stark contrast to his surrogate brothers.

I lifted my cheek up from his arm. My neck ached more than just when you fell asleep in a bad position. I ran my hand along my cheekbone, trying to remember what had happened. My fingers registered swelling and intense pressure. *The gun.* Igor had smashed it into my face when I tried to break loose from his hold. I pulled my hand away, searching for blood. There was a slight smearing of red, but it didn't seem excessive.

"You took a pretty bad beating from that cousin of yours."

I stared at Zayn, uncertain of what to say. He knew everything and must have thought the worst of me, just like I imagined Jai did. But his face didn't harbor any aggression. The only emotion I saw was the one I needed most right now—concern.

Directing my gaze to my lap, I blinked away the tears that heated my eyes. The weight of the day had finally descended on me, and I was afraid I'd crumble into pieces in front of him.

"I'm sorry. How long was I asleep for?" I asked meekly.

"Nearly twenty minutes," he said, studying me. "You were out cold. Barely dragged you out of that place before the entire building collapsed on us."

I gasped. The restaurant had blown up? "Where's Jai? Is he okay?" My heartrate skyrocketed thinking of him trapped under the rubble.

"He's fine. Nothing could kill that kid," he said, chuckling. "He's meeting us at my place in one of the other cars."

Exhaling a deep breath, I summoned the courage to ask what I already knew the answer to. "Leonid. Did he…?"

He shook his head. "He got away."

I stared out the window behind Zayn's shoulder. *Of course, he did.* Like Jai, he was immortal and an excellent liar. What did I do to deserve a life amongst dangerous men?

"Are you a spy for Leonid?" His question was so blunt that it yanked me out of my thoughts.

I locked eyes with him, so that he could see the earnestness in my reply. "Absolutely not." My voice was firm and full of conviction. I was on trial for crimes I didn't commit, and this was my last-ditch effort to make the judge believe me.

Zayn held my gaze, examining the depths of my eyes for several seconds. He was searching for signs that I was lying. The hum of the vehicle was the only sound between us.

At last, he issued his verdict: "I believe you."

Though I was grateful for his judgment, I was still skeptical. I certainly wouldn't have believed me if I were him. "Why?"

"I know what guilt looks like, and your eyes don't show any of it."

"What if I felt like I had nothing to feel guilty about?" I countered. "Leonid shows no remorse for any of his transgressions."

"True. But I saw the terror on your face when you were in his grasp. I know you're not working for him." The resolution in his voice sounded final.

I sighed, thanking God for his trust. If only I could make Jai understand too.

"Will you tell me your story?" he asked gently. "It sounds like it was one hell of a ride," he teased.

"That's putting it lightly." I couldn't help the soft giggle that escaped my lips. It felt good to smile. Just the mere wrinkling of the delicate skin around my eyes eased my nerves.

"Let's start with your name. Do I call you Karina now?" He enunciated each letter of my given name as if he were just learning to speak.

"No, Karina is dead. She is never coming back." I hated that name. It symbolized a life and a past that I wished had never happened. "Claire," I announced. "I am Claire."

"Okay. Claire it is." He nodded firmly. "How are you related to Leonid?"

I took a deep breath and then told him everything, spewing out words at warp speed. I told him how my mother married our father. I told him how Leonid killed my father and then,

28

years later, my mother. I shared how I ran away to the city, still assuming my new identity, and laid low until Leonid found me again.

He sat back in the car and listened intently, not showing much surprise or astonishment at the wild things he heard.

When I was finally finished, I collapsed back into my seat, taking a moment to catch my breath.

His eyes never broke contact with mine. "That was definitely a lot to unpack," he said.

"Can I ask you a question?" I asked.

"I think it's only fair, since I asked you to spill your deepest and darkest to me." He offered me a soft smile for encouragement.

"How do you know Leonid? I mean…he said you tried to kill him. Are you involved in the same …um…business as him…like selling people?" He had to be just as guilty of crimes as my brother was if they knew each other, yet from the moment I woke up next to him, I felt confusingly safe. I didn't feel the terror I felt when Leonid was near me.

My gut told me that he wasn't trying to kidnap me. I was probably too weak to fight him if he was.

"No. We don't traffic. Our business strictly involves the movement of drugs. We supply to the Bratva," he answered matter-of-factly.

I stared at him in disbelief. "I assume 'we' means Jai too?" I asked, the dread in my core burning my insides.

"Jai and Shyam technically own the business." His voice was gentle even though he was so forthcoming with answers.

My eyes widened even more. "Shyam too? But I thought he worked for Sethi Tech?" He always seemed like such a devoted husband and father. I would never have imagined he'd participate in the underworld like Leonid. What did Amelia think? Was she in on it too?

"He used to be the leader of the business, until he met Amelia and your father made a deal to have her trafficked on behalf of another adversary of ours."

My stomach turned with disgust. My father was a monster, and this just further reinforced that belief in my mind.

He continued, "But then, we cut him a deal so he would drop his mission to kidnap her. It worked, but Shyam decided that her life wasn't safe until he was completely out of this world. That was when he left it all to Jai."

I let the weight of his words sink in. "So, Jai is a kingpin?"

"No. Jai is the leader of the largest drug organization in the world," he corrected. "He *is* the drug world."

How could I have been so naïve to have seen this coming? I thought back to all those times that he evaded my questions about his job or gave me half-ass answers. *Exporting*?! I actually believed he worked in his father's business to export random goods like clothing or stupid knickknacks that you buy at large retailers for a couple of dollars. Never once did I imagine the goods to be drugs. How had I been so blind?

How did my brother play a role in all of this? "Why does Leonid hate him?" I wasn't understanding the connection.

Zayn rolled his eyes. "Your brother hates everyone. Leonid is still sour over your father rescinding his mission to kidnap Amelia. He didn't think the Bratva should compromise."

"How long ago did Papa agree to a ceasefire with Shyam?" I was desperate for as much information as I could get.

"About six years ago," he replied.

I considered the timeline. "Was this the reason Leonid killed Papa?"

He nodded grimly. "It would seem so."

*Jesus.* How could Leonid have thought to overthrow his own father just because of a deal he didn't agree with?

"If the Bratva finds out that Leonid killed Papa, they'll kill him." I had known the repercussions of Leonid's actions as soon as Maman told me he killed our father. He would have to pay for taking the life of a *Pakhan* with his own. I just wasn't brave enough to be the one who told the Brothers the truth. It was far too risky for me to have gone to them with this information. Maman never wanted me to speak of it again. If the Bratva didn't believe me, I'd have been as good as dead.

31

He rolled his phone in his hand as if deep in thought, "I'm betting on that."

My voice rose, mirroring my urgency. "We need to tell them!" I finally had another person to help me take Leonid down. Someone who knew how to fight and how to handle bad men like my brother.

He rested a hand on my shoulder to calm me down. "It's not that easy," he replied. "What if they don't believe us?"

That was my reason for keeping this secret for so long, too.

"Do you have proof of it?" I didn't have any proof other than the word of my dead mother.

"We do, but the Bratva isn't going to believe the likes of us. We have to play this smart. If we fail, they could always come after our family again."

My brows furrowed. "Again?"

He hesitated, as if wondering whether to speak his next words. "Why do you think Jai and Amelia were in that car accident?"

Realization dawned on me. Leonid was after Sethi blood.

I ran my hands through my hair, clutching at the roots. "God…I wish I had known all of this. I wouldn't have invited him back into your lives." I felt guilty for being related to that monster of a human and dragging poor Amelia back into this nightmare.

He tilted his head to the side. "How is this your fault? By falling in love with Jai? Leonid was already in our lives before he ever set eyes on you. If you ask me, you were the best thing that ever happened to Jai, despite who your family might be."

I turned away and rested my back against the seat, absorbing everything Zayn had just said. *You were the best thing that ever happened to Jai.* Actually, he was the best thing that had ever happened to me...until our lies caught up to us.

I had spent the past few years trying to free myself of the ties that had bound me to the underworld, only to find my way to its leader's bedroom.

The car slowed to a stop. I could see the exterior of what looked like a fancy hotel building. Six large glass panes set into two rows served as a window into the luxurious lobby. A grand chandelier that twinkled like constellations despite the distance hung from the middle.

"Not here. The garage," Zayn called out to the driver. With a nod of his head, the driver pulled back into traffic.

Catching the quizzical look on my face, he brought his fingers up to my cheek, lightly skimming my wound. It was starting to feel tight, most likely from blood coagulation. "No need to draw attention to us, right?"

I nodded. This place looked too classy for armed, oversized men and a woman covered in bruises and blood to be trudging through the lavish lobby.

33

"Is this where you live? A hotel?"

"My home is in India, but I moved here when Leonid started acting up. Jai needed reinforcements." He checked his phone and spoke as his eyes trailed from left to right, reading the notifications at the top of the screen. "I still need to figure out a more permanent living situation."

"Are you planning on staying here long term?" I asked. The change of topic from all things heavy was a nice change of pace.

"It looks that way." He tucked his phone back into his jacket pocket just as the car came to another stop. All traces of sunlight had disappeared under the haven of the cement ceiling. Zayn exited the car and walked around to my side to open my door for me.

"Thanks," I smiled.

He gave a soft smile before leading me through the industrial garage. The driver followed, spitting rapid-fire words to Zayn in a foreign tongue. The three of us entered what looked like a utility elevator. It must have only been used by hotel staff because it lacked any of the luxuriousness that the main hotel entrance boasted.

The two men continued to converse in whatever language they were speaking the whole way up. I stood in the corner with my arms wrapped around my core to steady my emotions over everything that had taken place today.

I suddenly felt tired. Tired of it all. It could have been the blow to the head or just that I genuinely needed a break from the adrenaline rush I had been suffering for years on end, but my eyelids drooped with overwhelming exhaustion.

The elevator binged and opened to a vestibule with a keycard reader next to a single door. Zayn scanned his card, granting us entrance.

My eyes roamed lazily over the grandeur of the penthouse that he called his "temporary home."

Marble floors, plush couches, and an expansive view of the city. *Do these guys ever reside in anything humble?*

Resentment washed over me. All that violence just for money. Fighting, lying, and cheating just for material things. So many innocent lives affected just for these men to get off on their power trips.

Even though Zayn seemed different than the others, he still chose to be a part of the underworld. He wasn't that much better than the rest, in my book.

Zayn dismissed the driver, who walked down the hall to the left of the living area, leaving us alone.

"You should sit down." He motioned to one of the oversized couches. "I'll get the first-aid kit for that cut."

Grateful for the invitation, I plopped down onto the seat.

I felt cold. It was the hottest part of summer, yet I was freezing down to my bones. I pulled the blanket that lay next to me on the cushion over my shoulders, willing my teeth to stop chattering.

Zayn returned, taking a seat on the marble coffee table in front of me. He had removed his suit jacket and undone the top two buttons of his crisp white shirt; the sleeves rolled up to his elbows. He seemed relaxed and at ease, and here I was, so on edge and unable to get warm enough, even under a thick chenille blanket.

"I put the heat on for you," he said. He nodded to my shivering mouth. "That's the shock. It's probably just hitting you."

He passed me a mug of what looked like light yellow tea. The warmth of the ceramic soothed my chill a little. "Drink up. It's chamomile."

I took a small sip, relaxing a little bit more.

Opening the little white case out onto the table next to him, he fished through it for supplies. He squirted some liquid onto a gauze pad and moved it up to my wound.

I blocked the pad from making contact. "You don't have to do this. I can clean it myself." I looked off to the side where the driver had disappeared moments ago. "Where's your bathroom?" I set my mug down and moved to stand, only to have him push my shoulders down, easing me back onto the seat.

I twisted my lips, annoyed at being bossed around.

He smirked. "Jai was right, you're as stubborn as they come." He pressed the gauze to my cut, and the sting caused me to suck air in through my teeth.

"As if he's any better," I gritted out. "Remember how he was after he bruised his ribs in the car crash?" He had been in denial that he'd been through a wreck and needed to rest. We'd had to scold him into taking it easy. The man thought he was invincible.

We chuckled in unison, finding humor in the man we both cared about. Yes, I still cared about him. I couldn't just forget my feelings for him despite the lies he had told me.

A beep sounded from behind the door, as if someone had scanned a keycard. The front door snapped open, and the echo of footsteps interrupted us. Zayn kept the gauze pressed to my laceration even as our heads turned. The smiles on our faces fell as we took in the inferno before us.

Threatening dark eyes pierced through the storm of tension he carried with him. His jaw was tightly clenched, as if he were gritting his back teeth hard enough to dent the enamel that coated them. He was a tall man by regular standards, but in this moment, he seemed even bigger, towering over our seated bodies. Thick red blood smeared along his jaw and fists only added to his terrifying presence.

"What the hell are you doing?" he roared at his brother; his eyes were glued to Zayn's fingers pressing the gauze to my cheek.

Coolly, Zayn finished dabbing at my wound, then discarded the pad onto the coffee table beside him. His expression remained even and unaffected. "Oh, good. You made it back in one piece. Glad you remembered to bring your key." Zayn nodded to Jai's pocket that most likely held the keycard he used to access the suite.

"Why the fuck is *she* here?" I had never heard his voice hold so much contempt. Karina, the little girl inside of me, wanted to divert her gaze in shame, but Claire, the woman I had become, refused to cower.

"I thought you'd want me to keep her safe until you got back." Eyeing the blood on Jai's chin, he continued, "Want me to clean that up, too?"

Jai's eyes flashed back to the cut on my cheek, his lips pressed tightly together. I thought I saw a hint of empathy for my wounds, but as quickly as it had appeared, it was gone.

Finally addressing me, he bellowed, "*Get out!*" with enough force to rattle my insides.

If that was all he had to say to me, even after all the love and passion we had shared, then it was best I left. I wasn't the only one who had kept secrets in our relationship, and I wasn't going to sit here and take his shit any longer.

Slipping the blanket off my shoulders, I placed it gently on the couch before pushing off the seat to take my leave. Before

I could stand, Zayn pressed both his hands on my knees, once again, signaling for me to remain seated. The gesture was brotherly, almost fatherly, yet it drew lasers from Jai's furious glare.

"*Bhaiya*, I love and respect you, but this is my home. Claire stays," he said calmly yet sternly.

That only incensed Jai more. "That's not even her fucking name. Were you not in that restaurant with me? How can you sit there like you weren't by my side, listening to her worthless brother spew the truth about her?" he shouted, his voice like thunder. "Are you a traitor like your *guest* and working for Leonid too?" He slithered closer, his eyes glowing with menace. "Maybe I should slit your throat to keep you from squealing to your boss."

From what little I knew of their relationship, Jai and Zayn were like brothers. They might not have been biological ones, but their bond was as tight as one made of blood. However, with how pissed he was, I didn't doubt Jai would do something irrational.

Zayn didn't seem worried at all. His thick body remained calm, unlike mine, which was so tense that my shoulders nearly touched my ears.

Unwavering, Zayn stood and approached Jai. The two men were around the same height, with Jai ever so slightly taller.

They faced off, simply staring for too long of a moment before Zayn spoke. "I think you should talk to her."

Jai sneered. "I have nothing to say to a liar like her."

It was one thing for him to put me down to my face but another to talk about me like I wasn't even in the room. Like I was someone so insignificant to him that he couldn't bother to speak to directly to me.

Zayn put his hands on his brother's shoulders, and Jai looked about ready to throttle him. "If not for her, do it for yourself." He leaned his face in closer to Jai and softened his voice like he was speaking to his son rather than his own peer. "*You* deserve answers.*"

He patted Jai, before turning back to me. "I'll be down the hall if anyone needs me."

The tension was stronger when it was just the two of us. He stood unmoving; eyes trained on me. It was clear that I would have to be the bigger person and start. How the hell did someone start a conversation like this? *I know I'm the half-sister of your sworn enemy and didn't tell you, but I don't work for the Bratva. You can trust me.* Yup. Terrible start.

I looked up at him. "Hey," was all that came to mind.

Silence.

I stood up and walked over to him, to finally face him, stopping about two feet away. The cut on his chin looked small,

40

yet the blood that had dripped from it was still shiny and red. It didn't look like it needed stitches.

The words came spilling out of me. "I wanted to tell you everything. I was going to tonight, but then I got a text from Leonid. I swear I had no idea about his involvement with your family or even that he was in town."

The vein in his neck twitched. Through clenched teeth, he growled, "Are you a spy?"

"What?! No." I moved in closer. Despite how much he scared me, my body still wanted to seek security in his. Before today, he had been my safe space, and my brain still registered him as that.

A sinister laugh, deep and low, rolled out of him, causing the hairs on the back of my neck to rise. Lowering his head to capture my eyes, he hovered so close that I could feel his warm breath brush against my lips. "If I had only known you were a Petrov, I would have put a bullet in that pretty little head right before you came around my dick." His hand moved to the curtain of hair around my face, held in place by dried sweat and the crusted blood that Zayn hadn't had a chance to clean off.

His thick fingers tucked an oily tendril behind my ear. He froze in place, his ominous smile withering away. The pad of his thumb smoothed over my cheek. Curious eyes examined the laceration that marred my skin. I was sure by now that Igor had left a pretty gnarly welt too from how sensitive the area felt. But I didn't care about the discomfort. I needed his touch.

My eyelids met each other, closing off my sense of sight to savor this feeling. My lips parted as I held my breath, too scared to make any sound that would scare off his tenderness.

His thumb swiped over my cut, sending my nerves firing with pain signals. I sucked in a harsh breath at the sting. My eyes flashed open, catching his dark brows knit together, wrinkling his forehead. His lips softened from the tight line they had been pressed into for much of our encounter so far, as if preparing themselves to speak the words that swirled in his heart.

Grasping the backs of his hands as they remained softly clasping the sides of my head, I pled with him. "Please, Jai. You have to trust me. I would never do anything that you're accusing me of. I love you." Despite his deception, I still loved him. I just couldn't erase our history that easily.

His eyes flicked from side to side as if trying to read my thoughts. I closed the distance between us, pressing my lips softly against his. Tears trailed down my cheeks when I closed my eyes. He remained unresponsive to my kiss, yet he didn't pull away. He was conflicted, as was I. None of this was easy for either of us, but the fact that he wasn't pushing me away was all the invitation I needed.

I moved into his frame, pressing the front of my body against his. Parting my lips, I nipped his lower lip between mine, using the tip of my tongue to skim the full, smooth flesh. Tastes of cinnamon salted with the taste of my tears danced on my tongue. His mouth finally parted on its own. The rigidness of his length pressed into my belly, sending irrational waves of heat pulsing to my sex. Arousal was the last thing we should be feeling in this moment, but it was the reassurance we needed.

This thing between us could weather any storm that threatened to separate us. Neither Leonid nor the Bratva could break this chemistry. Our attraction was too strong, and I had faith that our love was even stronger.

I needed more of him...more than this timid kiss. My tongue plunged into his mouth, devouring him. My hips pressed forward to find the friction I was so desperate for—to forget all our problems.

Suddenly, the lips I was trying to seek refuge in were ripped away from mine. Thick hands wrapped firmly around my throat, his grasp testing the limits of the pressure it would take to close off my airway. My head tipped back as I watched fury storm his dark eyes. My hands clawed at his, trying to pull them off my neck.

He threw me backward, away from him, releasing me from his grasp. Stumbling to catch my balance, I clutched at my neck in shock.

"How the fuck do you expect me to believe you?" His voice was shaking with rage. "I trusted you!" he screamed, his hands pulling at his hair. "I will never believe another word that comes out of your mouth, *Karina*."

The sound of my birthname on his lips seared a hole in my chest. "Don't call me that," I hissed.

The wicked gleam in his eye returned as he realized that he had pressed the right button. "What's wrong, Karina? Upset that I know who you really are? A lying…Russian…whore." Each word singed the open wound in my heart.

Bright red clouded my vision. "Fuck you," I cried. Digging my heels into the ground, I glared at him. I had seen his irrational side before and knew that when he was in this mode, he would fling insults like ammo until I backed away. And even though I didn't want to claim my father as my own, no child of Nicholai Petrov would lay like a doormat and allow anyone to degrade her. I had too much self-respect to take his shit anymore.

Startled by my outburst, Jai gaped at me.

"You think you're so fucking innocent in all of this? A victim?" I yelled. My shoulders shook from the anger coursing through me. "You're the fucking liar. Yes, I kept secrets from you because I was running for my life. What about you? The great drug lord!" I flourished my hand in the air as if he was some great emperor waiting for me to bow to him.

Inching closer, I narrowed my eyes on my target. "Tell me, how many innocent lives have perished under your hand? How many victims have died from overdose from your products? Do you think you're better than Leonid? As I see it, you're just as bad, maybe even worse. Stringing women along for your amusement, giving them a false sense of security, meanwhile you spend your time bartering with monsters like my brother. At least everyone knows who Leonid is and how evil he is. But you...you're the devil in disguise. A fucking imposter."

His nostrils flared with hatred and his hands balled into tight fists at his sides.

"Go ahead, hurt me. I fucking dare you." I knew he wouldn't really do it. He was all show, and I was fed up with his theatrics.

His body succumbed to rage, and he let out a howling cry so deep that it rumbled my core.

"I think it's time for you to leave." Zayn had appeared. He stood straight as a rod as he glared at Jai.

I crossed my arms over my belly to keep my insides from exploding from all the adrenaline surging through me.

Without turning his head away from his brother, Zayn addressed me. "Claire, you'll stay here under my protection until we figure out what to do about Leonid."

My eyes stayed trained on Jai as I gave a reluctant nod. I didn't want to intrude in Zayn's life anymore than I already had. I had involuntarily pinned him against his brother, but I didn't have anywhere to go. The second I returned to my apartment, Leonid would be waiting for me with a one-way ticket to Kazan.

Jai scorned, "Oh, now you two are best friends?" Accusation filled his eyes and his brows lowered and pinched in disgust as he looked at me. "Are you fucking him, too?"

Hot tears overflowed in streams down my cheeks. My stomach clenched with disbelief. Before I could defend my honor, Zayn's roaring voice sounded again. "Get the fuck out of my house, *brother*."

Without a hint of regret, Jai gave me one final glance before turning on his heel and storming out of the suite. The door slammed with a thunderous crash, leaving me feeling more alone than I ever had.

# CHAPTER IV

## JAI

M y eyes burned from staring at my monitor for the past three hours in my office at Nirvana, the club I owned with Shyam. Exhaustion from lack of sleep didn't help my situation either. I wanted to shut my laptop and take a break, but I needed to learn as much about the Petrov family as I possibly could.

Piecing information together was difficult since the Bratva were discreet about family matters. Most everything I had found were things I already knew and centered on Nicholai and Leonid. There was virtually no data on a Karina Petrov nor her mother.

47

My research was interrupted by a fat manila folder slamming onto my keyboard sending a string of z's streaming across the document I was using to take notes.

"What the fuck, man?!"

"You should have done this before you stuck your dick in her." My brother's face dripped contempt. He thought I was careless for not having investigated her before fucking her. It had always been his protocol to conduct thorough background checks on any person he came within five feet of. Hell, he had even vetted his own wife when they first fucked.

I had never thought it was necessary. No woman had ever lasted longer than one night, and if they ever became clingy, I had my men do the dirty job of dumping them. I hadn't realized how immature I had been until I met *her*.

God, I didn't even know what to call her. *Karina* just felt foreign to me. But that was just it—*she* was foreign to me. *Claire* wasn't Leonid's sister or the daughter of the Bratva. She would always be the first woman that I had loved—and the last. *Claire* was dead to me; I had buried her deep in my cold heart.

Fingering the thick file, I braced myself for what was inside, then flipped the cover over and scanned the reports.

"You know you could have just emailed this to me, right?" I said, bouncing from line to line of dizzying facts.

Standing in front of my desk, he tucked his hands into his pockets. "Yeah, but it's far more dramatic to do it this way. Plus, more of an opportunity for me to say, 'I told you so.'"

I wanted to knock his arrogant self off his high horse. "You didn't tell me shit about Claire. If I remember correctly, you said she was 'agreeable.' You and your wife were practically pushing me to hook up with her."

"Correction: I said her *looks* were agreeable. I never said anything about her as a person," he continued with his know-it-all voice. His judgmental glare drilled into me, trying to teach me a lesson, like I was one of his kids. "How would I know what she's really like without a background check? How could you even think to trust someone without doing some research first? Would you buy a used car without knowing its history first?"

What the hell did he know about buying a used car? All his cars had been specially made for his royal highness. "She's not a Kia, asshole. Normal people don't run checks on everyone they meet!"

"But *we* are not normal people." He took the seat across from my desk. "I ran one on Amelia and look at how well we turned out."

"Well, she didn't run one on you, and she's the better part of you." And far less neurotic than him too.

He put his hands up in defeat. "I won't disagree with that."

"You're lucky she stuck around with you despite your paranoid, psychopathic tendencies."

"Whatever." He shrugged. "It's better than using Myspace to vet the girls you want to screw."

I screwed up my face. "Myspace? How the fuck did we elect you as the CEO of Sethi Tech?" It was a wonder that a dinosaur like him had been a co-founder of the most successful tech company in the world.

"Say what you want, but I have job security. It helps that I'm sleeping with the Chief Technology Officer." He flashed a sly smile.

"Gross." The last thing I wanted to think about was my brother and sister-in-law having sex. I needed to bleach my brain later.

Shaking the images away, I rolled my eyes. "I think you better get your application ready for a job at one of those arts and-crafts-stores run by some little old ladies."

"At least I never fucked with the Bratva…literally," he shot back.

I felt sick all over again remembering all the lies I had ever heard from her mouth. I had fucked my enemy's sister. I had been played for a fool and the entire underworld was probably laughing at my weakness.

I had brought this woman into my life. She had been around my family. How long had she been planning her move to infiltrate us? A spy would surely masquerade as a dance teacher for children to get to me. Was she responsible for the car crash that nearly killed Amelia and me?

Shyam had been outraged when I told him everything, and rightfully so. The Bratva had once wanted to kidnap his wife, and now that they knew he had children, Meena and Dylan would surely be on their hitlist too. His home was protected by armed guards around the clock. Amelia and the children were no longer permitted to leave the house. I couldn't imagine how they'd broken the news to the kids, especially Meena, who was completely attached to her *ballet teacher.*

I dropped my gaze in shame, unable to face my brother's probing stare. My fingers flicked through the pages in front of me. "Let me guess. You read this already?"

He steepled his fingers in front of his lips. "Of course, I did."

Scanning the documents, I read much of what I already knew. Leonid and Igor had murdered Nicholai, later blaming his death on an accidental car crash. Claire had even told me as much, but at the time, I hadn't suspected she was talking about Nicholai Petrov.

Leonid soon assumed the role of *Pakhan* of the Bratva, as his Brothers had no clue his hands were stained with his father's blood. Nicholai had been their beloved leader and his murderer would be their enemy.

Over the next few years, Leonid covertly hoarded arms in warehouses all over Lebanon and hid money from his Brothers in various untraceable accounts across the Middle East with the help of one of the most notorious crime families in Lebanon.

Something new caught my eye. "Leonid is Nicholai's son from his first wife?"

Shyam nodded.

I read further. Apparently, Leonid's mother had a long-term affair with a soldier behind his father's back and was hanged for her crimes in front of her only child.

"Turn the page," Shyam ordered.

I looked up hesitantly at my brother. The expression on his face told me that I was in for some heavy shit.

I flipped the page and read on.

Nicholai soon remarried. A French woman by the name of Camille, no maiden name. There wasn't much listed about her past except that she was from southern France.

"How did you find this out?" I had been looking up data for hours and hadn't read any of this.

He grinned. "Not too shabby for an *old man*, huh?" he mocked me.

My eye caught the name I had been most interested in. Karina Petrov was the only child of Nicholai and Camille. She was born when Leonid was barely a teenager.

No one in the underworld knew that Nicholai had a daughter. He had kept her a secret. Maybe it had been the shame of having a daughter instead of a son. Or maybe he had done it to keep her safe. The players in our world were evil and would stop at nothing to decimate and degrade the property of a leader. There was no bigger act of supremacy than to rape the daughter of an underworld kingpin.

My stomach churned at the idea of anyone touching her. Even though I hated her, I couldn't shut off the side of me that still cared about her. When I saw Igor trying to kidnap her from the restaurant, my heart lurched in my chest and all I could think about was getting her away from him. And when I saw the wounds that he had inflicted on her face, I was ready to find him and rip his heart out with my bare hands.

It was the same feeling I had when I saw Zayn step into the role I once held. Walking in on them as he tended to her wounds and made her laugh, had enraged me. Their intimacy had been like a bullet to the heart. How could the love of my life and my brother have been so comfortable after only a few meetings? Zayn must have been under her spell too. I had fallen for her charms, and now he was stupid enough to make the same mistake.

It would explain why they were huddled close in the living room and why he was so quick to offer his home as shelter to her. If he wanted her that bad, then he could have her. I was done with her Bratva pussy.

Even though I was so disgusted with her, I would never forget the torment I felt last night. She had lied to me, yet I still wanted her. Feeling her body so close to mine had made me lose all recollection of why I was angry. As shameful as it was to admit, her lips were the only medicine I needed in the moment to numb my grief, and oddly enough, they were the reason for my anguish. My body had responded in the only way it knew how to when she pressed into me. My dick betrayed my brain and twitched from the feel of her tongue on me.

I was even more pissed that she had witnessed my moment of weakness. I fucking hated Karina.

Shyam waited patiently as I refocused my thoughts and continued where I had left off in the file. He knew this was a lot for me to take in and tried his best not to hurry me.

"After Nicholai's death, his wife and daughter went missing?"

"They ran away to France," he answered even though the next line of the report clearly stated it.

I rubbed the scruff on my jaw. "Why?"

"Because of Leonid. He had planned to kill his sister next so that nothing stood in his way when he succeeded his father."

"And Leonid never found them?" He was diabolical and would have stopped at nothing to locate Karina and her mother.

"He tried. But they had changed their identities. Nicholai's wife became Sylvie Varon, and his daughter became—"

"Claire Varon," I whispered, completing his sentence.

"They ran away by themselves?" I couldn't imagine how the wife and daughter of a former *Pakhan* could escape without the help of others to ensure their safety.

Shyam hesitated before answering. "Mikhail helped them get away."

Mikhail—my Bratva informant. He was one of the oldest members of the Bratva, having been there when Nicholai first became *Pakhan*. He was well respected, and his opinion held weight. However, in recent years, Leonid had done everything to suppress Mikhail's power and respect.

I had never doubted his loyalty to me since his hate for Leonid was so strong, but it was far too coincidental that he tipped me off on Leonid's whereabouts just when Karina would be there. Leonid seemed to know the details of my relationship with his sister and maybe Mikhail did too, even though I hadn't ever disclosed any of that information to him. Was this all just one big set-up where I was the only one who was clueless?

I had some words to share with my informant.

I closed the file and gripped the edge of my desk. "Set up a meeting with Mikhail."

# CHAPTER V

## CLAIRE

Zayn's hotel suite was beyond luxurious. The five-star accommodations boasted every amenity that could possibly be desired in a living situation, or in his case, a temporary living situation. But even under the ridiculously high thread count sheets and with three overstuffed down pillows stacked under my head in the dark, I couldn't get comfortable.

Last night wasn't much different, either. I was most likely in for another four hours of tossing and turning before I crawled out of bed to put on a full pot of coffee in hopes of keeping my brain functioning at a minimum of fifty percent capacity.

I missed my own apartment. The chipped beige paint and scuffed trims that, if I had to guess, were once a bright shade of white. The beat-up television that I had found on consignment, held together by duct tape. The tattered quilt on my bed that so desperately needed to be patched up with a needle and thread. I needed familiarity to comfort me right now, and nothing in this suite was remotely familiar.

Zayn was more than gracious to allow me to stay here. I had felt awkward when he extended the invitation, especially since I barely knew him. My only interactions with him had been in the presence of Jai or Amelia. But there was something about him that I trusted. He was one of those people who radiated such clarity and honesty that I knew he had my best intentions at heart. Returning to my place was out of the question while Leonid was still on the loose.

After minutes of protesting his offer and explaining that I didn't want to be in his way, especially since his offer only added fuel to Jai's fury, I had accepted. He'd assured me that I wouldn't be intruding, and he had been right, judging from the spacious guestroom I was staying in. It even had an adjoining full bathroom, complete with a slipper tub.

I should have felt lucky to stay in a room like this and treat myself to every luxury it had to offer, but instead, I spent most of my time replaying the events after the showdown at the restaurant.

I couldn't understand how Jai's anger had sliced my heart in half, yet the feel of his body against mine still made me feel so protected. The way his brow had creased with worry when he noticed my cheek, and his caress had made me forget it all.

Touching my cheek just the way he had, I could feel the swelling that accompanied the deep blue bruise that had appeared. I skimmed my fingers along the curve of my jaw, brushing them against my lips. The brief taste of his lower lip hadn't been enough. I had needed more of him before we dealt with the shit storm between us—one more moment of unrestrained abandon.

The warmth of his mouth when I had plunged my tongue inside only heightened my need. My lips tingled in the dark solitude of my room. Biting my lower lip to lessen the sensation, I wished away the desires that swirled inside of my head. But they wouldn't leave. The memory of Jai's spicy scent surrounded me, urging me to keep going. My fingers glided down my neck, trailing to the top button of my pajama top. Shaky fingers unbuttoned each one slowly, until my breasts were finally free of their restraint.

I remembered the feel of Jai's fingers circling my nipple, spreading goosebumps over my core. I teased myself like I knew he would have, tracing the circumference of my areola, making my nipple peak. Pinching my fingers around my erect bud sent rays of pleasurable pain shooting through me. The feeling was so heavenly that I couldn't hold back the moan that vibrated in my throat.

I froze when I realized how loud I was, listening through the stillness for any sign of Zayn near my door. He wouldn't enter my room without knocking, and the place was so massive that he probably hadn't heard anything at all. But still, I waited to be sure that the coast was clear, because the longing was still strong.

My hand kneaded my breast, as my back arched into my touch. Sliding lower over my belly and playing at the waistband of my cotton sleep shorts, I slipped my hand inside and made my way down to my clit. I remembered the way his tongue used to feel lapping at me. My fingers toyed against the smooth flesh, building tension.

Fever took over my body, suffocating me under the sheets. My legs kicked until the blanket scrunched up at the bottom of the bed, leaving me exposed to the night. My hips lifted high enough for me to slide my shorts and panties down, giving me full access to the neediest part of my body.

My fingers worked in quick, tight circles as my hips moved with the same rhythm. "Jai," I moaned loudly into the silence. *Fuck!* I slammed my free palm against my mouth to hush myself.

My frenetic grinding was evident by the soft knocking of the headboard against the wall. I slowed my paced slightly to keep from waking up the penthouse, only to slip a finger into my wet pussy. My walls missed Jai's thick cock. I remembered how big it had felt pressed against my belly on my first night here. One of my fingers couldn't compare to his size. Three fingers plunged inside, sending arousal trickling down my hand.

My index finger of the hand over my mouth slipped between my lips, triggering my sucking reflex, the same as when Jai would slide into my mouth. I wanted so badly to taste his salty stickiness, to be milking his shaft with my tongue.

Jai's face appeared over me, as I fucked myself relentlessly with my fingers. His deep, sexy voice groaned out, "Baby girl," filling my ears and making me moan around my finger.

Wet sounds filled the air as I broached my edge, assaulting my hole. Only a moment more and I'd be...

*"Lying...Russian...whore."*

The memory of his words drenched my pleasure in ice water. My body tensed with rage. I remembered it all clearly. His fists clenching. His degrading words. His hand around my neck. I fucking hated him.

The man who was supposed to love and respect me thought of me in the same way as my sociopathic brother. They were two sides of the same damn coin, and they could both go fuck themselves.

Pulling up my underwear and pants, I flung myself to sit on the edge of my bed. I breathed deeply, trying to bring my respiratory rate back down.

I stood up and grabbed the robe on the chair by the window, using it to cover my pajamas. Letting out a heavy sigh, I started out of my room to put on a pot of strong coffee. *Guess I'll be starting my morning before the sun rises today.*

\*\*\*

The lack of sleep was really getting to me. Lying on my stomach on my bed, I fought to keep my eyes open as I tried to read a book. The words would blur together right before my lids fell heavily over my eyes. My body would relax, only to send my head tipping over my perched hands, jolting me awake each time. Except the last time, I was startled awake by a knock on the door.

I sat up and adjusted my bra to fully contain my breasts under my shirt. Zayn had been nice enough to have the hotel concierge buy me some clothes. It was still warm outside since it was the tail end of summer, so most of the options were blouses and wrap dresses. The concierge must have thought I was way more sophisticated, judging from the formality of the pieces.

The underwear the shopper had chosen were also fancier than what I was accustomed to. Tons of black lace pieces that barely held my bits in place. Anytime I bent over, the cups of the bras shifted, and my nipples threatened to pop out. And I didn't even want to get started on the panties. I walked around with a constant wedgie from how skimpy the bottoms were, even moreso than the stretchy thongs I owned. These weren't underwear, they were *lingerie*.

Zayn had asked me for my clothing and shoe sizes to give to the concierge but never my underwear size. That would have been too awkward and personal to share with a man I had lived with for all of five minutes.

"Come in," I called out.

Zayn poked his head through the door. "Hey. Busy?"

He was a good-looking man. From my understanding, he was the "middle brother," according to age. Jai, like Shyam, was tall and lean, yet his muscles were cut and finely chiseled, screaming their presence even under clothes.

Zayn was bigger than both men. His frame was buff and ripped, like that of a bodyguard. From the neck down, he was lethal. But his face didn't carry the sternness that Jai's and Shyam's did. His expressions were light and full of earnestness. His dark hair was a little longer than his brothers', but not too long where it looked unkempt. His features, like his square jaw and full eyebrows, could have made another person look severe, but with his sincerity, he just seemed kind. Though, I was sure he was more deadly than his brothers when tested.

Any awkwardness I had felt staying with him had disappeared after the first night. He gave me ample privacy and was courteous when I ran into him in the kitchen or hallway. His sense of humor was the most charming thing about him. It wasn't the sarcastic kind that gave a person an edge, but more a means to entertain the company around him. That was it. He was considerate.

I shook my head. "What's up?"

"You have a visitor." He opened the door a little wider.

"Lana!"

She came running over to me on the bed and pulled me into a tight hug. "Girl! Where have you been?"

I gave her one last squeeze before pulling away. "You know. Around." I fidgeted with my hair, tucking loose tendrils behind my ears.

"Woah! What happened to your face?" she hovered her fingers over my bruised cheek. The wound had started healing over and I didn't need a bandage anymore.

I covered the area with my hand, self-consciously. "Oh, it's a long story. I'll tell you everything later."

Smiling, Zayn interrupted us. "Let me know if you two need anything," he said before shutting the door. He must have called Lana and told her where I was staying so she wouldn't worry. I was so grateful that he allowed my friend to visit me during this lonely time.

Lana turned back to me with wide eyes and fanned herself. "He's hot!"

"Shut up. You think everyone is hot." I playfully shoved her shoulder.

Excitement bubbled inside of me because my friend was here. I had never been so glad to see her long dark hair and oversized, innocent-looking brown eyes. On her small, delicate face, her features made her look almost childlike, even though we were around the same age.

Her outfits made her seem even more like a cartoon character. An aspiring fashion designer, Lana made most of her clothes, and each of her outfits were *unique*. Today, she was sporting a neon- yellow blazer, heavily adorned with gold medallions like a yacht captain or some shit, which she'd paired with a nude-and-black plaid mini skirt and white tank.

"Why didn't you tell me you were shacking up with a fucking Roman god?!" she exclaimed.

"Indian," I quickly corrected. "We're not shacking up. He's Jai's brother."

"Huh?" She scrunched her face up. "How did that happen? He looks nothing like them."

"He's not biologically related. They just grew up together."

"Oooh," she sang as she tipped her chin up in the air. "So, why are you living here, again?"

I sighed. "Why do you have so many questions?"

"Maybe I wouldn't if my best friend ever called me! Where were you the other night? You bailed on me, and I never heard from you again." At first glance, her pout looked exaggerated and fake, but I knew it was real. That was just Lana. Everything about her was amplified.

"It's a long story." I looked down at my hands in my lap to avoid her glare.

Lana kicked off her chunky patent-leather chunky heels and leaned against the headboard like she was getting ready to watch a movie in bed. "I got time."

I slid up alongside her, leaning back to get comfortable since we'd be here for a while, and started from the beginning.

For what felt like hours of talking, Lana sat transfixed by the wild tale that came rushing out of me. When I was finished, I took a fortifying breath as she stared, dumbfounded, at me.

I smacked her on her knee to shake her out of her shock. "Say something!"

Shaking her head in disbelief, all she could manage was, "Wow!"

"Do you hate me for lying to you?"

"What? No way." Resting her hand on top of mine on my lap, she gave it a gentle squeeze. "I just need a minute to process all of that."

"I get it." It was a lot to dump on a person, so she could take all the time she needed. It was surprisingly easier to recount everything after having told most of it to Zayn already.

Practicing on him had helped me to choose the right words when confessing everything to Lana.

"So, where is your brother now?" she asked.

I shrugged. "I don't know. But that's why I'm staying here with Zayn. The minute I go back to my apartment, he'll be waiting for me."

"Have you spoken to Jai since you lost it on each other?"

I shook my head.

She crossed her arms over her chest, wrinkling her nose up in disgust. "Good. He's an ass."

I swatted her. "Lana! Keep it down." Although he wasn't on speaking terms with Jai, Zayn was still his brother, and I didn't want him overhearing us badmouthing his family. It was disrespectful especially since I was a guest in his home.

"Whatever, Zayn thinks he's an ass too!" she shouted loud enough that I was sure Zayn had at least picked up his name.

I broke out into a giggle, with Lana following.

"Laughter looks good on you, friend." She gazed at me, her expression soft.

"It *feels* good." It definitely broke up the monotony of worry that I experienced much of the day.

"It can't be easy being stuck in here all day, alone with your thoughts." She hopped off the bed and went over to the floor-length mirror to fluff her hair up.

67

"It sucks." I admitted. I should have felt lucky to be hiding out in such a lavish shelter instead of a dingy cargo truck this time around, but it still felt like a prison. "I'm exhausted from my thoughts racing at night."

"I wasn't gonna say anything, but you do look like crap," she teased me through her reflection in the mirror.

"Jerk!" I threw a pillow from the bed, aiming for her ass, but she dodged out of the way just in time. Reveling in her victory, she stuck her tongue out at me in the mirror.

"So, when can I bust you out of here for some fresh air? There's this party that Craig invited me to. You should come." I guess that meant her relationship with Craig, the bouncer from Nirvana, was still going strong.

Zayn had given me strict instructions that I wasn't to leave the hotel suite. He had his men guarding the place twenty-four hours a day, forbidding anyone except hotel personnel to enter under their careful watch. He had even posed as my cousin and had called the director at the ballet studio to tell him that I would no longer be instructing due to a family emergency. "I'm not allowed to leave."

"What? Is he just going to keep you locked up in here forever?"

"Just until they catch Leonid."

She let out a whistle. "How will you get laid?"

I snorted. "That's the last thing on my mind right now." She didn't have to know how last night's fingering session had turned into a disaster. Even in his absence, Jai was ruining masturbation for me. *Merde!*

"Maybe you should take advantage of living with that hunk out there?" She wiggled her eyebrows as her lips fixed into a mischievous smile.

"Who? Zayn?" I nearly choked on my spit. "No way!"

"What's wrong with him? He's nice, gorgeous, and ripped like a fucking gladiator!" She licked her lips like she was ready to devour a five-course meal.

Zayn really had the whole package; except he wasn't right for me. I wasn't remotely attracted to him because memories of his brother still haunted me. "I'll pass."

"Suit yourself." Lana shrugged. "So, wait. What do I call you now?" she asked.

"Claire. I want to be known as Claire. I don't like the memories that Karina stirs up for me."

She nodded with understanding. "I get it. Claire it is."

Her eyes roamed over my head, examining me. I could sense the wheels turning between her ears. "You should go back to your natural hair color."

"What?" I said fingering my light blonde hair.

"You said it was honey colored, right?"

"Yeah…," I answered skeptically.

She assessed my locks as if planning her best coloring strategy. "I think you'd look better with darker hair," she said.

"Gee, thanks!" I rolled my eyes. "Way to tell me you hate my hair!"

"I don't *hate* it. I just know it comes from a bottle. You're not the processed type."

"Well, seeing as how I'm not going anywhere anytime soon, I doubt I'd be able to make it to the drugstore in time to lighten up my dark roots." I hadn't been able to touch up my color in a long time and my natural hue had blanketed my scalp, giving my hair an uneven tone.

Lana gasped with excitement suddenly. "Oh-em-gee! I have the most amazing idea."

I smiled nervously, knowing that whatever she had in store for me couldn't be good.

# CHAPTER VI

## CLAIRE

"**W**hat the fuck did you make me do, Lana?" I whispered as I inspected the drastic change before me in the mirror. Atop my furrowed brow, my darker-colored hair fell in whisps over my forehead.

I hadn't seen this much of this hair color since I was a teenager. Sure, it wasn't exactly 'natural' yet, but it was as close to my real color as I was going to get. It also fixed the hideous issue of my roots showing through light blond hair.

Lana had been hell-bent on me going to whatever party her boyfriend was invited to ever since she'd mentioned it days ago. I was aware of the type of "events" Craig frequented, and they weren't my thing. But I had been locked up in this golden tower for nearly a week now, and I was damn near losing my mind.

My daily routine still consisted of nights of tossing and turning with my thoughts, then rolling out of bed prematurely to caff up, which subsequently left me jittery and anxious about my entire life, until the sun set, and I did it all over again. My brain was my own personal hell, and there was no escaping it. Not while I was stuck in this gilded birdcage.

I had no one to talk to and my cellphone had been confiscated by one of Zayn's men. They were worried that Leonid would use it to track my whereabouts. And I had no room here to dance, nor any of my pointe shoes. My body felt foreign to me when it wasn't in motion.

Random visits from Lana were my only mode of escape from the hurricane of shit flying around in my head. She had been gracious enough to pick up my birth control from the pharmacy so I could continue taking them, even though I wouldn't be having sex anytime soon. I was trapped with virtually no one to see, let alone hook up with. It was lonely as hell.

So, when Lana came up with a plan to break me out of here for the party, I had foolishly jumped at the chance. Armed with a box of honey-colored hair dye and scissors, she had shown up to give me a new look this morning. Bangs framed my face and flowed into layers that gradually lengthened as they made their way around my shoulders.

I stood staring in awe at the woman I saw in the mirror. She looked older than twenty-one and shrewder than her bright blonde counterpart. It could have been from all the shit that had happened over the past week and the wrinkles that had formed around my eyes from lack of sleep. In any case, the change was noticeable. My bright blue eyes even shone a little darker, grayer, with the change in hair color.

I checked the time on the bedside clock. *7:59 P.M.*

Lana's instructions were clear: Be ready to sneak out at 8 P.M.

Craig would come to the door right at eight disguised as hotel security. With his size and serious face, he would be believable. He was to give Zayn's guard the run-around as he spewed some crap about noise complaints. Once they left the doorway and were out of sight, I'd sneak my way out.

Zayn had left earlier with a crew of his men, as he did most days, and hadn't returned yet. He probably wouldn't be back for hours.

Lana had secured me a disguise to wear over my party clothes, a black dress and white shoes just like the maids wore. I would haul ass and make my way downstairs before any surveilling guards noticed me and meet Lana outside of the garage. There, she would have a change of shoes ready for me.

I'd been skeptical when she explained everything earlier today before heading out to get herself ready, but as time ticked on, I was now convinced this was the dumbest idea ever.

VICTORIA WOODS

I was ready to call the whole thing off when I heard the guard's voice. I creaked my door open to listen in and could hear Craig in the distance, responding in his gruff voice.

Footsteps.

They were walking away. Now was my time. I checked both directions in the hall before sliding out of my room and closing the door quietly. I walked quickly to the front door, my white shoes falling softly on the floor. Thank God for that.

My heart pounded with exhilaration as I neared the door. A moment of freedom was within my grasp. I gripped the handle, amazed that Lana's hair-brained scheme might actually have worked.

"Where do you think you're going?"

I jumped and let out a yelp as my hand clutched at my chest over my heart. Turning around, I found Zayn's hard form standing a few feet away from me. His arms were crossed over his chest and his lips were set in a smirk, as if he were just waiting for whatever amusing story I was planning to feed him.

I saved the theatrics and decided to fess up. I would just have been insulting Zayn's intelligence by lying. "Don't be mad. I wanted a night out to clear my head."

He eyed my ridiculous outfit. "Dressed like a maid?"

My fingers fiddled with one of the oversized buttons close to my belly. "I figured a disguise would help throw Leonid's men off my track."

"And my men too?" He stepped closer, studying my face. His fingers smoothed a flyaway hair around my face. "That would explain the hair too." His fingers lazily twirled a tendril. "Did you do this yourself?"

I swallowed the lump in my throat. The interrogation made me nervous as hell. Shaking my head, I replied, "Lana."

"She's got some skill. It looks good on you." He let go of my hair and pushed his hands into the pockets of his jeans. His black t-shirt was stretched across his thick chest, outlining every mound of muscle he had.

My neck suddenly felt hot under his scrutiny. "Thanks."

"Sir, we caught this man posing as a security guard."

One of Zayn's guards had the collar of Craig's white polo shirt in his clutch. Craig looked ready to rip the goon's throat out. I took in his get up, complete with a black tag with "SECURITY" written in white letters.

How the hell Lana had scored his disguise too amazed me. Glad to know she was putting her fashion degree to good use by styling people appropriately for escape missions.

I giggled at the ridiculousness of all of it.

Six pairs of eyes stared at me in surprise.

Zayn's eyes twinkled with amusement. "What am I missing here? Do you know him?"

I nodded through tears of laughter. "He's Lana's boyfriend. A bouncer at Nirvana."

Zayn flashed back to the intruder in the security-guard outfit and sized him up, then turned back to me. "Where were you guys running off to?"

"A party that Lana is dying for us to attend," I answered.

"A party?" Zayn asked Craig.

"Yes, sir," Craig replied in his baritone voice. "We were just heading out to have some fun and then we'd return Claire by morning."

Zayn stepped in front of me so close that I could feel his breath on my skin. "I told you not to leave the house."

I looked away from his protective glare. "I know. I'm sorry. I just needed a break from being trapped in here."

"Trapped?" he asked as if I had somehow offended him.

"That's not what I meant," I corrected myself hastily. "I'm so grateful that you've opened up your home to me, but I spend so much of my time just thinking about *things* that I think I'm starting to go a little crazy."

"You know I can't let you out alone before…" He turned to look at Craig, unsure of how much he knew. "Something happens," he finished.

"I know. You're right. It was a dumb idea." It really was. The fact that I had believed I wouldn't get caught was even dumber. Yeah, I was fucking losing my mind.

I stepped around him to return to my room. "I'll head to bed. Good night."

"Come on. Let's go."

I looked at him in confusion. "Where?"

"To this party," he said and motioned to the door.

I shook my head in confusion. "But I thought it was unsafe."

"Nothing will happen to you if you're with me, and I'll bring my men to make sure of it."

I felt my cheeks hurt from the wide smile that spread across my face.

"Hurry up and lose the maid's dress. Lana must be panicking right now because her best friend and boyfriend have gone missing."

I nearly skipped like a child to my room to remove the hideous costume, too thrilled to contain my excitement.

# CHAPTER VII

## JAI

All Bratva brothers in New York and back in Kazan were under lockdown since Leonid had retreated. This meant that Mikhail was going to be under careful watch too. I hadn't seen him when we ambushed Leonid at Semya, most likely because he'd been standing guard at the perimeter of the area. Whether he was protecting Leonid or me, was still up for debate.

I needed to see Mikhail to get to the bottom of his fidelity and hear answers to the questions that had clouded my head.

All reports indicated that Claire…or Karina…or whoever… was just another casualty of her brother's need for power, but I couldn't be sure of her current relationship with her brother.

Were they on speaking terms? If so, how long ago had they reconciled?

Blood was thicker than water, and who was to say that she didn't have inherent loyalty to him? Family members often fell out of favor only to reunite stronger than ever. I couldn't be sure of her motives. I had no choice but to wait until Mikhail was free from Leonid's watchful eye.

I sat in the dark hotel suite stewing in my thoughts. The deep bass of the music vibrated my seat. Usually by now, I would have already been in the privacy of a bedroom upstairs having my way with a new piece of ass, or two. But tonight, like a king on a throne, I oversaw the bacchanalia that was taking place.

All furniture had been removed and replaced with lush couches. All lights had been cut except for the overhead black lights that bathed the area in a violet sheen. Platforms had been erected along the perimeter, each large enough for a dancer to work the pole stationed in the center. They twirled effortlessly in nothing but special black-light body paint that glowed in neon colors under the lights as onlookers lusted after them.

Partygoers filled the center, grinding sensually on one another to the beat of the music. I watched from my throne on the highest platform, with red curtains drawn halfway so I could see through but still maintain my distance from the orgy happening on the floor.

Women, young and toned, writhed on the floor, their bodies undulating only for the eyes of their admirers. The men all worked for me in some capacity, whether they were guards or bouncers at Nirvana, so I could trust each one of them in this safe space.

I leaned back in my seat, taking in the scene. My eyes fell on a few women I thought were attractive, but they stirred nothing inside to prompt me to invite them over. This party was meant to take my mind off *her*, but instead, it was just reminding me of my lack of desire for someone new.

Too distracted by thoughts of my ex-girlfriend, I didn't notice the half-naked brunette slithering her way up to my platform. Her gold string bikini outlined her petite, fit body. The hungry look in her eye was fierce enough that even the darkness couldn't dampen it. Reaching the final step before entering my private enclave, she placed a hand on my thigh and gripped it tightly to pull herself up.

My body remained motionless and my eyes speculative of her intent. Her hips undulated in circles to the steady beat, giving me a front row view of the rhinestone charm above her belly button. Swirls of neon purple, green, and pink painted on her belly attempted to entrance me.

As she bent forward to bring her face close to mine, her dark hair tickled me. She smelled like fruit candy, so sweet that

81

it made my stomach turn. Biting her lower lip playfully, she slid a hand over my dick to feel for any effect she might be having on me. I watched her eyebrows narrow ever so slightly as she registered my lack of interest. Like a pro at maintaining a poker face, she quickly relaxed her brow, hiding any of her bewilderment. She probably thought she was hot enough to get any man hard and dripping for her. *A very wrong assumption.*

Spinning quickly around so her back was facing me, she perched her tight ass on my thigh, rubbing her pussy against the denim on my quad. Even though my booth was partly concealed, I was sure the entire dance floor could see the "private" show I was receiving. Leaning back onto my shoulder, she writhed against me, tossing her hair as she worked me.

I stared with boredom into the crowd, just in time to catch a familiar face in my line of sight—one that I had grown up with. Flanked by his men, Zayn's presence turned every head.

He had some balls to show up here. How had he even found out we were having this party?

He ducked his head to whisper into the ear of the woman beside him. The lights were too dim for me to make out much of her features, but whatever he had said elicited a smile from her, showing her bright teeth. Her white halter dress shone just as brightly as her smile, clinging to her curves.

I clenched my hand so tightly that my knuckles felt ready to burst through the skin as I watched Zayn and his date enjoy the party I paid for. My brother, now my enemy, wasn't welcome here. Shouldn't he have been home minding his new Russian friend?

I watched Zayn guide his date through the crowd with his hand on the small of her back. Recognition dawned on me as they moved closer to my platform. My whole body stiffened with bitterness as my companion continued bouncing her ass on my leg, oblivious to the inferno blazing to life inside of me.

I barely recognized her with her new hairstyle, but it was her. She couldn't hide her grace, even in this crowd of oversexed people. The way her back remained straight and her shoulders never slouched. The firm curvature of her plump ass. I remembered all of it. My dick sure as hell remembered, as it too betrayed me by coming to life.

Another woman a little shorter than her handed her a shot glass, which she happily accepted before they clinked their glasses and downed the liquid in unison. This must have been her friend Lana, from what little I could make out.

Lana pulled her friend across the dance floor, into the thicket of grinding bodies. Zayn moved with them, barricading anyone from touching them.

I watched her dance with reckless abandon, her hips swaying to the music. Her arms floated into the air overhead as she really got into it, the outline of her muscles flexing rhythmically.

Every man looked ready to devour her. She looked free and happy, which only set my teeth grinding against each other. Her carefree vibe pissed me the fuck off.

Zayn moved beside her, brushing her hair away from her ear as he leaned his mouth in again. My hand flew to the arm of my lap buddy, gripping it hard. Letting out a yelp of pain, she jumped out of my lap, knocking loudly over the music into one of the posts that held the drapes in place and drawing the attention of the crowd. All eyes were on me as I locked eyes with the person who had stomped my heart into pieces.

Without thinking, I stormed off my platform and down the steps to the dance floor. The sea of people parted, afraid of being scorched by my wrath. The only people who didn't move were the two who were most unwelcome.

The music continued, hiding the beastlike snarl emanating from my chest as I approached her. "Leave!" I shouted, audible even over the loud booming of the speakers.

Holding her ground like I had anticipated she would, she simply shook her head, never releasing me from her gaze.

Considering this his invitation to get involved, Zayn inserted himself between us, crossing his arms over his chest like he was a cement wall of protection for her.

My jaw tightened at his audacity. When had he become this person who would stand against me? There was a time when he would have stood by me unconditionally. Apparently, things had changed.

He might have been a trained fighter, but my temper was far more destructive than he could ever be. My chest inflated as I stepped in closer, ready to strike. His glare was unyielding as I hovered my face right in front of his, my top lip rolled into a snarl.

Long, thin fingers pressed into the skin on my bicep, dragging me away. All the way back on the platform, she released her grasp with a final fling of her arm. After drawing the curtains shut, bathing us in even more darkness and privacy, she turned on me. I could feel the outrage that seethed off her, even if I couldn't see it clearly.

The party volume decreased into moderate background noise.

"What the fuck do you think you're doing? That's your brother out there," she scolded. "Don't confuse your hate for me as hate for *him*."

I hated them both. This, I was most sure of. The unwanted proximity and seclusion only heightened the pain I carried in my chest when I remembered how we used to be. Pain followed by disgust was the sequence of emotions that constantly cycled through me.

"Stay out of matters you know nothing about, *Karina*." The emphasis on her real name triggered something feral inside of her and the whites of her eyes grew bigger.

"Don't call me that," she hissed.

I grabbed the only moment of enjoyment I'd had in about a week and ran with it, taking an even cheaper shot to mute my own heartache at seeing her again. "Do you only like when Zayn calls you by your Bratva name, *Karina?*"

In one quick movement, she lunged at me, gripping my jaw, her nails digging into my skin. Her face was so close to me that I could feel her warm breath. Her sweet smell of strawberries mixed with the pierce of her sharp talons embedded into my face fucked with my head in the best way possible. She personified the storm of contradicting emotions that raged inside of me.

My hand shot to her wrist, causing her to whimper at the crushing pressure I inflicted, and effectively loosening her grip on me. Pinning her hand behind her back, I used my free hand to yank her hair by the roots at the back of her head. She was at my mercy, right where I wanted her. Right where she belonged.

Our mouths smashed into each other, the passionate hate for each other fueling our hunger. My tongue delved past her lips, searching for hers as I held her head in place. Her eager tongue danced against mine, pleading for me to give her more.

86

My lack of sight did nothing to diminish my arousal. If anything, it only served to make it stronger. All my other senses were magnified, shutting out any protest my conscious brain might have supplied.

Walking us backward, I shuffled until the backs of my knees touched the chair before pulling her down onto my lap. Our desperate lips never broke contact.

Her legs straddled me, her knees resting on either side of my hips. I knew she could feel the raging hardon that was achingly growing beneath my jeans.

Soft hair fell wildly over my face, sometimes getting caught between our lips in the sticky mess of her lip gloss and our saliva. My fingers pushed the tendrils back so that my hands framed her face. Bites alternated with kisses as our mouths moved like they shared a mind of their own.

Even the way her hands clutched my t-shirt was forceful, reminding me that this wasn't a moment of desire for either of us. No. It was an instance of primal need. When I should logically have been shoving her off me like any other lying bitch would have deserved, I was instead pumping my hips up to meet her clothed pussy.

The grinding motion was successful at having her tear away from my mouth long enough to moan her approval. Her back arched as I gripped her hips to rub her against me. The strokes were long and hard, enough to maximize contact with her clit. I needed her good and wet for what my cock wanted to do to her right now.

My hands followed the outline of her halter strap behind her neck. I pulled on it, hoping to release however it was held together, but no luck. She always had a knack for wearing shit that was impossible to remove.

Ducking her head, she helped remove the strap as I slipped it over her, releasing it to fall in front of her chest, dangling free. I pulled the rest of the fabric down enough to free her breasts and massaged them as the humping intensified.

My head lowered as I felt for her nipple with my tongue, laving the firm peak and enjoying her squirm under my touch.

Raising onto her knees, she dipped a hand between us to undo my fly. I lifted my hips to shift my pants down, freeing my eager dick. Chilling sensations streamed from the head downward, as precum dripped from my tip.

My fingers found the fabric of her panties. *Lace.* My mind strayed to where she must have gotten such an expensive pair of panties. *Not now, asshole!* But I couldn't keep from pondering who must have bought these for her, especially if she still couldn't go to her apartment to get her clothes because of Leonid.

Blood rushed through my ears as I pictured Zayn holding them up for her to try on. Like when the first sprays of an ice-cold shower hit an overheated body, I snapped back to reality. My hands shoved her hips to nudge her off my lap.

Instead of heeding my demand, she fisted my cock, pumping twice to coat precum along my shaft, effectively stunning me into submission. Without giving me a chance to argue, she hovered herself over me, using my tip to move her panties aside. The small stroke along her swollen flesh caused my cock to jerk in appreciation. Then, she suddenly slammed herself straight down my length, drawing low moans from both of us.

I hadn't been with anyone since we had broken up, but I couldn't say the same about her with certainty. I didn't care right now. There was no turning back now, not even if I tried. I was seeing this fuck through until the end, with nothing between us. I wanted Zayn to smell my cum when he tried to get near her pussy tonight after they left. I marked her sex as mine.

Her arms hooked around my neck as she rode me hard, hitting the tip of her cervix every time she descended. I gripped her tight ass as she fucked me with expert precision.

The slapping sounds of her ass against my thighs only spurred us on to quicken the pace, and I flexed my hips up to hit her even deeper. I wanted her to feel pain every time she walked tomorrow, to force her to think of how she had betrayed me. And from the way she moved, she wanted to punish me by fucking my dick raw. *Good. Glad we finally found something in common.*

Her pussy tightened around me, the vise grip choking my length. Her tits smacked my face as she worked me. Our groans and moans had grown louder, but I didn't give a shit as long as I was the only one who got to see her this wild. The whole damn party could listen in if they wanted to…to hear how I owned her pussy.

I was ready to burst, and she must have felt it too. "Jai," she moaned out as her hands clutched my hair, holding on for dear life.

"Claire," I blurted out without thinking. The name had fallen out, even though I had sworn never to use it again. In the heat of everything, it felt like the old days, when I would call out that name all night as we made love.

"I love that name on your lips," she managed to say through her quickened pants. "Say it again."

My brain told me to say no. To call her Karina again just to piss her off. But my heart…my heart caved. "Claire, I'm gonna come."

"*Mon dieu,* Jai. Yes." She went crazy on me, thrashing around as her walls squeezed me in pulses, her body shaking with release as her scream filled my ears. I exploded into her soon after with a guttural moan that sounded more beast than human.

Her body slumped over me as our breaths slowed, and our fluids mixed into a mouth-watering combination of sweet and salty. The music had at some point during our tryst grown louder and the sounds of chatter had resumed.

Maybe they had heard us. Maybe they hadn't. But I was sure as hell that Zayn knew what I had just done to her, and that gave me all the satisfaction I needed.

She pulled off my almost limp dick and wordlessly readjusted her thong and the hem of her dress. Then her white halter neck slid over her head and back into place. The form of her dress looked as it had when we first came onto the platform.

"Thanks," she purred out in her sweetest tone laced with sarcasm. Then she turned around and exited through the closed curtains as if nothing had happened, like she didn't have my cum sliding out of her warm pussy, leaving me astonished and alone with my soft dick.

# Chapter VIII

## Claire

I had used him. It had felt good for the five minutes it took to slip out through the curtains and find Zayn to tell him I was ready to go home. But the euphoria had worn off as I sat in the car, staring at the city lights zooming by out my window. It must have been the endorphins that were responsible for the initial hit of confidence I had experienced as I sashayed out of the suite like I had just made Jai my bitch.

Now, in the void of the chaos of the party, loneliness took hold again.

Lying on my back as I stared up at the ceiling in my room, I simmered in regret. I had never hate-fucked anyone. Last night was the first time, or at least, it had started off with feelings of hate. Somewhere in the midst of it, they had been replaced with the type of need that I always felt when we were together. I didn't know if he had felt the shift too. After that last wave of bliss had left my body, the bitter reality of what we were had returned to me, and I'd refused to let him have the upper hand again. It would have been so like him to discard me and walk away like I was trash. So, I did it to him before he ever had the chance.

It was a stupid mistake. For all I knew, he could have bedded a new woman every night since we broke up. I was disgusted with myself thinking of what viruses I had possibly exposed myself to. The thought also broke my heart. *How many women had he fucked since me?* He had always been a playboy, and it had been naïve of me to think he wouldn't revert to his old ways.

From the looks of the party he had thrown, Jai was back in commission. I guess, I just thought he'd have held out a little longer.

I should have at least made him wear a condom. *So stupid.*

Everyone in attendance knew we had fucked behind the velvet curtains, even Zayn. He had been silent for most of the drive home, only asking me if I was okay when we strapped on our seatbelts.

Lana knew it, too. She had high-fived me for being the first to exit the platform "like a boss," in her words. She said it was good that I'd reminded him of what he had lost. But all I kept thinking about was how much *I* had lost when we broke up.

It still fucking hurt. I had thought sex would ease some of the pain, but it had only made it worse. The truth was, I just hadn't been able to resist one more time with him, no matter how much of an asshole I thought he was.

I should have felt unsafe with him. He was just as dangerous as Leonid. I scorned my body for its need to be near him, even now as I lay in bed. I was turning into one of those fucked-up women who pined after their toxic ex-boyfriends, and it repulsed me.

I needed to distract myself from my new full-time job of self-loathing. Jumping off my bed, I left my room in search of something to eat for lunch. Voices sounded in the hallway, one thick and deep that belonged to Zayn, and the other...higher pitched and feminine.

I halted just around the corner, out of view, to listen before deciding if my quest for lunch would have to be postponed.

"We all miss you. You haven't been over to see us in far too long," the woman said.

"You know I can't visit. I don't want to come between brothers," Zayn's voice sounded.

The female voice grew louder. "*You* are their brother, too!"

"Jai won't even speak to me, and I'm sure Shyam is just as pissed, since it's been nothing but radio silence from him too," Zayn argued.

I rounded the corner quickly, seeing just who I had expected. "Amelia," I gasped. I hadn't seen or heard from her since Leonid came back into my life, obliterating it into pieces. And from the look on her face, she knew everything.

Her naturally doe-like green eyes stared at me for a second. I didn't read hatred or distaste in the lines indented across her fair forehead. Instead, her expression seemed hesitant more than anything. As if she were unsure of how to proceed.

Her eyes flashed nervously to Zayn and then back to me. Tucking her red hair behind her ears, she took two steps in my direction, still more than an arm's length away, like she was afraid to get any closer.

"Hey," was all she managed to say. Her fingers intertwined with each other, fidgeting in front of her stomach.

"Hey," I replied, crossing my arms over my chest, feeling overly self-conscious of what she must have thought of me.

"I like your hair," she said, tipping her chin up to indicate my darker style.

Fingering my hair, which I seemed to be doing a lot lately as I adjusted to my new look, I awkwardly replied, "Thanks."

Releasing her hands, she dropped them to her sides. "Can we talk?"

I nodded at the chance to explain my side to her. No doubt she had heard it all from Jai's point of view, and her opinion of

96

me mattered. I still considered her a friend, and I wanted to chance to speak for myself.

"If you ladies will excuse me," Zayn interrupted. "I have some work to finish up." He placed a hand gently on Amelia's back, smiling at both of us reassuringly, before making his way down to his office.

Amelia moved to the living room and took a seat on the couch. I sat on the opposite end of the same couch, turning my body to face her.

Based on her lack of eye contact, I knew she was struggling to find where to begin, so I took the lead. "I'm sure you heard everything."

She caught my line of vision, looking as if my stare might burn her. "Um…yes."

"Do you hate me like Jai does?"

She shook her head, taking me by surprise.

"But I lied to you." I had thought for sure she would be upset that I had kept all of this from her.

"I understand why you did it," she admitted quietly.

My eyebrows shot up. "You do?"

She bobbed her head up and down, swallowing before speaking. "When I first met Shyam, he didn't tell me what he really did for a living. I thought he just ran a tech company and was hiring me to fill a position."

97

I knew some of her history with Shyam and his initial involvement in Jai's business from what Zayn had shared with me, but I let her speak.

"I soon found out that he hired me to help him track down an enemy in India, named Tarun. He had raped and killed Shyam and Jai's mother."

I moved my hand to my mouth to stifle my gasp. He had never told me this. My heart ached for him because I knew what that pain was like to carry around. Losing a parent to the hands of a murderer was never easy.

She continued, "Tarun was basically living off the grid in India when we tried to locate him."

"Did you find him?" I asked.

She nodded. "I was able to figure out the coordinates of where he was, but..." She paused for a moment, taking a fortifying breath. "But before I could tell Shyam, he kidnapped me all the way to India." Her voice broke, and I could see tears forming in her eyes.

Before she could say another word, I slid to her side of the couch and placed my hand on her knee. I wanted to ask if he had hurt her, but I didn't want to pry for any more than she was willing to give. "How did you escape?"

"I left breadcrumbs for the boys. They picked up on my clues and ended up finding me."

"And they killed Tarun?"

"Yes. But he hadn't been the only threat wanting blood," she replied carefully.

I knew where she was going with his. "My father."

She nodded. "You knew about the deal?"

"Only from what Zayn has told me. I didn't know the details of Papa's business. I just knew that he was a bad man."

"Were you close to your father?" she asked.

"No," I replied. "Maman and I were more of an inconvenience to him than his loved ones. And to Leonid, I was just a threat to his new empire."

"So, you really had no clue about their involvement with Shyam and Jai?"

I shook my head fervently. If I had, I would have steered clear of Jai.

Tears started leaking down her face. "If anything ever happened to my kids, I wouldn't be able to bear it. Leonid can take me if he wants, but I just want him to leave my children alone." Her voice shook with anxiety.

My stomach twisted thinking about my connection to the demon who was possibly planning to harm Meena and Dylan. "I swear to you, Amelia, I will not let anything happen to those children." I didn't know what Leonid had in store for me or the Sethis, but I sure as hell wasn't going to let him harm a hair on those children's heads.

She swiped at her tears as I held her gaze. "I believe you," she said.

I smiled, grateful for her trust.

"I know what it's like to be a captive of an evil man, and when I look into your face, I can relate to what I see. I see the hurt and the stress that comes with it."

I understood what she meant. I identified with everything I saw scribbled on her face, too.

"I also know that of all the Sethi brothers, Zayn has the best sixth sense about people. He knows when people are lying, so if he trusts you, then I trust you."

"Does Shyam believe me?" I asked nervously.

"He's skeptical…to put it nicely."

I don't know why I would have expected Shyam to believe me, but I felt upset that he didn't.

"He doesn't know that I'm meeting with you today," she said.

"What? How did you pull that off?" I knew she had been under twenty-four-hour guard because of the lack of knowledge of Leonid's whereabouts.

"I told the guards that I had my period and that I'd rather drive myself to get supplies. They realized too late that I wasn't headed to the drugstore, so now they're waiting outside Zayn's door." Her face lit up with a proud smile.

I chuckled. "I bet Shyam is on his way over here as we speak."

"I wouldn't be surprised if he was, either." The light smile on her face faded. "I know that your brother was responsible for Nicholai's death, but did he have anything to do with your mother's too?"

I didn't respond, except for the tightening of my lips. She understood my meaning.

"God, I'm so sorry…wait, what do I call you?"

"I prefer Claire," I said.

"Noted."

"I have no proof," I continued. "But I know Leonid was responsible for her death. He admitted as much to me."

"Have you gone to the police about this?" she asked.

I gave her a hard stare. "You know the police are in our world's pockets." The underworld ran everything, and the police didn't dare get involved.

She leaned back on the couch as if a weight had just fallen onto her shoulders. "I guess it really is *our* world, no matter how hard we try to distance ourselves from it, huh?"

"It's unfair. I didn't choose to be a part of this damn world." I felt myself getting angry all over again. I just wanted off the carousel of men sizing up each other's dicks.

Understanding radiated over her simple features. "Neither did I. That's why I understand why you hid your past from us.

At first, I was upset, and I felt betrayed. But I had never shared any of my history with you because I didn't want to bring that into your life, especially since I wanted nothing to do with it."

"I get it." I didn't feel at all slighted that she hadn't told me about Shyam's past.

"But Jai should have told you," she continued, pointing a finger at me to show how serious she was. "We even urged him to tell you early on, but he never did."

"I think he was planning to the day I met with Leonid, but then all hell broke loose. I was certainly planning to tell him my past that day."

"Secrets and lies will only ruin you," she said, more like a prophecy than as a response in conversation.

"I'll cheers to that." I raised my hand in the air, pretending I had a drink in it.

"Have you seen or spoken to Jai at all?" she asked.

I chose my words carefully, not wanting to share too much. She was still his sister-in-law, after all. "Kind of."

"What does that mean?" she asked.

"I saw him last night."

"Where? Did he come here? Zayn didn't mention that!" She perked up, bubbling with excitement. "That's such a huge step for Jai."

"No. I ended up going to a party with Lana and Zayn that we didn't know he was hosting."

102

Her brows furrowed. "Zayn went too?"

"Yup."

"How did that go over?" I could tell she was bracing herself because she knew something had happened between the two men.

"Terrible." I sighed. "Jai almost punched him."

"Oh, God. His temper is something else. Both Shyam and Jai are like bombs just waiting to detonate. What did Zayn do?"

"He remained calm but didn't back down."

"Yeah, he's like that." She looked over to the hallway to make sure he wasn't standing there before continuing. "It takes a lot to set him over the edge."

"I can tell." Throughout this entire situation, Zayn had kept a cool head in the face of Jai's explosive and irrational behavior. I was initially worried that I would pit brother against brother by staying with Zayn, but honestly, I hadn't felt any animosity on Zayn's end.

"Zayn was actually the one who found me when I escaped from Tarun," she offered.

"Really?" I gasped.

"Yeah. I thought he was one of Tarun's thugs capturing me again, but I was wrong. I will forever be indebted to Zayn for helping me. He's really an amazing human being."

I smiled. "I completely agree."

Her face grew serious, and she paused before speaking again. "I have to ask this, and you can totally tell me to shut up and mind my own business, but are you interested in Zayn?"

I nearly slid off the edge of the couch. "What?"

"Judging from your reaction, I'll take that as a no."

This time, I scanned the perimeter of the suite myself to make sure Zayn wasn't in earshot because it would be even more awkward if he were around to hear this embarrassing conversation. Lowering my voice, I explained my surprise. "Don't get me wrong. He's a nice guy, but I'm not attracted to him."

It was the truth. Zayn was sweet and protective, and insanely good-looking, but I didn't see him that way. The lack of attraction made it easy to stay at his place without worrying about things getting complicated. I wasn't ready to move on, either, as evidence by my actions last night. Jai still clouded my brain.

"Wait a second," I said hastily, stopping her before she could respond. "You don't think he likes me, do you?" Oh God, I hadn't even considered that possibility.

"No, I don't think so. He doesn't seem to be into you in that way. Although, I've never seen him with anyone, so I guess I wouldn't know how he acts when he's interested."

I rolled my eyes, chuckling. "That's not reassuring at all!"

"I do know that he wears his heart on his sleeve, and if he were into you, he'd have let you know from the beginning."

Well, he hadn't told me anything of the sort or led me to believe he was interested. The knots in my stomach relaxed a little more.

"But Jai thinks he's into you," she warned.

"Ugh, I know. It was part of the reason he acted like a caveman last night."

She covered her ears with her hands. "Ohhh, I'm actually picturing it in my head, and I feel so sorry for you. What happened after he tried to punch Zayn?"

"I pulled him away to stop him before he did something stupid…"

"And?" She perched her chin on her hand, waiting for more details.

I debated on whether to say anything. But Amelia already knew more than I wanted her to know about my personal life, so why bother hiding anything now? "And then *I* did something stupid."

"No!" she exclaimed.

I nodded sheepishly.

"But I thought he was still angry at you?!" she asked.

"He is! And I'm still pissed at him."

"Ohhh…angry sex!" She winked at me slyly.

I shushed her. Zayn already suspected we had fucked, but I didn't want him to know specifics. We were friends but not that good of friends. "You can't tell anyone."

"Please, who am I going to tell? Shyam?" She snorted.

Imagining Shyam gossiping over who his brother had slept with was so ridiculous to me that I burst out laughing too. "Good point!"

After our laughter settled, Amelia continued, "How do you feel now?"

I shrugged. "I still can't stand him, but I can't get him out of my head."

"I completely understand that. You had a past with him and opened your heart to him. It's going to take a lot of time to get over him…if that's truly what you want." Her eyebrow lifted as I pondered her words.

"I don't know what I want," I said after several moments. My voice sounded hollow and empty.

"I don't think he knows either," she offered.

"Really?" That surprised me. "He seems absolute in his decision to break up."

"He's impetuous and does shit without thinking. But I know he's still stuck on you because he only goes so hard for the things he's passionate about. And he was passionate about you before you guys ended things."

My hands fidgeted in my lap. "He's just so…mean right now."

"Unfortunately, that's the bad part about being with a Sethi brother. When they're pissed, they're ready to burn down the house just to keep you out of it."

"Is Shyam that way with you?" I was curious to know about their dynamics at home.

"Not anymore. When we were dating, he was very bullheaded and thought he was the boss of me. Now, he still likes to think he's the boss, but he never loses his temper on me."

"Probably because he knows you're the real boss!" I giggled.

"Shhh. Don't let him know that." We both cackled loudly.

"I see both of you ladies are having a hell of a time, but Amelia, your husband is ready to send a small militia to get you." Zayn approached us, his smile suggesting that he loved the light-heartedness he was hearing in his home.

"Oh shit, he called?" Amelia asked.

"And he's pissed," he confirmed.

"Crap, I better get home and deal with him."

She placed her soft hand over mine. "Claire, if you need anything, just let me know. I'm here for you." Her bright smile warmed my tired heart.

"Thank you," I smiled back. She pulled me into a quick hug before releasing me to go over and hug Zayn goodbye.

"And you, don't be a stranger," she said, holding onto his large biceps. "Come over. We need to hash this out, once and for all."

"Yes, ma'am," Zayn saluted her as if she were his general or something.

"Bye, guys," she said and waved from the door.

"You show 'em who's the real boss," I shouted after her, earning a wink before she left to deal with her very own angry Sethi brother at home.

# CHAPTER IX

## JAI

"Why the fuck is she taking so long to get home?" Shyam was livid. I hadn't seen him so pissed off over something Amelia had done in, well...forever. She had always been the perfect sedative to his indignant side. Sure, he still got irritated over small things, but it was always over something stupid, like when the maid fucked up his laundry or the waitress gave him anything less than top-shelf scotch, and none of it was directed toward his wife.

"Shoulda kept better tabs on your woman," I teased smugly, knowing he hated it when I offered him unsolicited advice.

I grabbed an apple from the fruit bowl in front of me, then I turned around and hoisted myself up onto the counter, tossing the shiny fruit in the air and catching it with my other hand. Raising it to my lips, I took a bite, only to be greeted by a twinge of pain shooting through my tooth and radiating through my gums.

My face wrinkled in disgust at the bitter, processed taste lingering on my tongue. "What the hell is this?"

Shyam glanced at his watch in annoyance. "Decorative apple, genius."

"And you let me eat it?" I threw the apple across the kitchen, where it landed in the oversized stainless-steel sink with a racket. "What's the point of having a crystal bowl full of fake fruit? Where the hell is the real fruit?"

"Will you shut the fuck up about the damn fruit?" he barked, slamming his hands on the counter next to me.

Just then, footsteps sounded on the polished floors. "What's going on here?" Amelia stood in the entryway eyeing her husband, who looked nearly ready to combust.

"Why did you go over there alone?" Shyam's voice was harsh, more like he was her father rather than her husband.

Although I knew he had a penchant to overreact when it came to Amelia's safety, I agreed that it had been completely foolish of her to be alone with Claire. If Leonid had come for her again, Amelia wouldn't have been able to avoid his clutches.

I jumped off the counter, ready to talk some sense into her, though I was fairly sure she was about to get one hell of an earful from Shyam.

"What do you mean?" She approached us, sliding the strap of her purse over her head. She walked around us impassively and placed her bag on the counter, making us both turn completely around to face her. Classic power move—make everyone in the room focus on you while you act like you don't give a fuck.

"You knew I didn't want you alone with that woman," he answered, his tone so sharp it could cut metal. Shyam was losing what little patience he had left. I knew what would happen next when he got like this. Anything within arm's reach would be fair game for him to catapult across the room.

Taking note of the shift in his behavior, I slid the fruit basket out of his reach.

Pinning her fists to her hips, Amelia was not having any of what Shyam was serving. "One, we weren't alone. Yours and Zayn's men had the place flanked." She looked away and quickly analyzed the displaced fruit bowl with more interest than she paid her husband. "And two, where did the ninth apple go?"

"Enough!" Shyam roared, filling the whole room with his anger. Even my arm hairs raised slightly from the force of his voice. Thank God the kids were with the nanny in the basement playroom. "You defied my orders. I told you to stay away from her!"

Amelia snorted. "I *defied your orders?* Are you really coming at me with that bullshit, asshole?"

Shyam's spine stiffened, and his jaw clenched. Shit was about to hit the fan.

She stalked forward, passing me, with only him in her field of fire.

"You don't get to tell me what to do. I'm a big girl and I can take care of myself." Poking her finger into the center of his chest, she carried on, "I'm your wife and your equal. Not some minion who works for you and jumps to lick your ass whenever you give an order."

In the blink of an eye, Shyam grabbed her wrist, twisting it hard and forcing her to bend over the counter as she cried out in surprise.

I jumped back in shock, watching as he secured one hand behind her head and pressed it onto the marble. His other hand had somehow caught hold of both wrists, keeping her from moving. She struggled against him, shouting for him to let her go.

I sprang into action, pulling on his arm that held her wrists, trying to loosen his hold. "Shyam, let her go! She's your wife!"

His temper was bad, but I hadn't thought it was bad enough to punish his own wife like some abusive piece-of-shit husband. Our mother had raised him better than this!

112

"That is exactly why I'm doing this," he ground out, unrelenting in his hold. "She's my fucking wife," he screamed.

Oh, God. This was bad. So bad.

"Let me go! You're hurting me!" Her voice was shaky from crying. She tried butting him with her ass.

I tried to keep my voice steady, even though I was panicking inside. "Shyam. Stop it!"

As quickly as he had captured her, he let her go. Backing up from her, he watched her with eagle-eye focus, like he was ready to strike again.

Amelia spun around, vehemence wild across her face as tears still flowed from her eyes. "You son of a bitch!" she yelled. Her breathing came out ragged in between the last few sobs as she attempted to settle herself.

"Shyam, what the hell is your problem?" I fumed.

"She is." He jutted his chin out in his wife's direction, then looked directly at her. "You think you're so tough? You couldn't even break free from me—what makes you think you could handle Leonid?"

I found it to be way too extreme, but he had a good point.

"Is that what this was? A fucking lesson? To make me fall into place?" she huffed out incredulously.

"No, this was to show you the danger that you and our kids are in by associating with the Bratva," he spat.

113

"Have you fucking forgotten that I'm already aware of the type of danger men like you can inflict? And Claire is *not* the Bratva!" she cried.

I saw the flicker of guilt pass through Shyam's features, but he ignored the jab in reference to his past. "You can't be sure of that. Do you not remember the shit that Nicholai wanted to do with you? And now we have children! How do you know she's not feeding Leonid intel about us?"

Launching at Shyam, she shoved him hard in his chest. "If you had fucking talked to me like an adult, I would have told you how earnest she was when I met with her."

"She's faking it," I interjected. Even though I had kept replaying images of her riding me last night, I couldn't let go of my mistrust of her.

"Like you should talk about trust?" she seethed, coming for me next.

Baffled at how quickly she had turned this around, I asked, "What the hell did I do?"

"You're just as guilty as she is in this. Did you really think keeping your work from her was going to end in happily ever after?"

"It's my personal business and I choose to share it whenever I want," I argued.

114

"Yeah, and how did that work out for you?" She tapped her foot, waiting for my answer.

I just stared at her dumbstruck.

"And she could say the same, you moron!" she continued when I didn't respond. "She's over there hurting just like you fucking are because of the lies that the both of you told one another. You're not innocent in this. You're lucky that she even cares about you after all you put her through." Her words rushed out, matching the frantic pace of her hands moving in front of her.

But I only registered one part of her entire lecture. "She still cares about me?"

"You're a bigger idiot than Shyam." She flashed another angry glance at her husband, who shifted uncomfortably at his wife's lashing. "Of course, she still cares. And you're still in love with her, too, otherwise or you wouldn't be using every chance you get to turn the knife in her heart."

Moving closer into my space, she set her sights entirely on me. "Do you know the shit she went through as a kid? She never asked to be born into the Bratva, just like I never fucking asked to be involved with your shady-ass business! You men just get off on money, power, and control at the expense of the women in your lives. Nicholai did it to Claire's mother. And even though he didn't mean for it to happen, Shyam did it to me."

Shyam lowered his head in shame, probably playing through all the danger he had exposed Amelia to during his reign over our empire.

"And you"—she pointed her finger in my face— "you did the same thing to Claire. She's a fucking human being. She spent most of her teenage and adult life running from men like you. Cut her some fucking slack for not telling you about her past. She was too busy trying to survive under Leonid's radar."

"How can I be sure she's not working for them? Blood is thicker than water. Relatives fall out all the time and come back together stronger than ever." I wasn't fully convinced she was a victim of Leonid's crimes.

"This isn't some family squabble over Thanksgiving!" she bellowed. "Her life was endangered, and her own brother had put a target on her head. Wake up! She's the real victim here, and if you still give a shit about her, you should be working to protect her instead of letting Zayn do it for you."

"Don't talk to me about him." He was a traitor, and I couldn't forgive him.

"As far as I see it, Zayn has been way more of a man than you have during this entire situation. Have you ever known him to be a bad judge of character? He saw what I saw in her...the fear and trauma that she suffered...and he did what any real man would do and protected her. He's doing *your* job!"

116

My gut churned as the brutal honesty of her words seemed to break something in me open. She was right—I had fucked this up so badly that my relationships with Claire and Zayn were probably beyond repair. Amelia had planted the seed of doubt in my belief of Claire's guilt.

"And you," she said, turning back to Shyam. "You haven't even checked on Zayn to see if he needed any help with security? Instead, you left him out there to fend for himself. What kind of brother are you?"

"*Jaan*, I'm sorry. I was worried about your safety. You're the love of my life, and I would die if anything happened to you." He neared her and took her hands in his, examining any damage he might have caused her wrists when he assaulted her.

"You have a stupid way of showing it," she muttered, but let him tend to her wrists.

"You knew I was an ogre before you married me." A smile with a hint of boyish charm spread across his lips.

"Yeah, well, I think it's time for a change." She cocked her chin up defiantly.

"I'll do anything for you. Name it." This was the Shyam I knew. Completely pussy-whipped by his wife.

"Make up with Zayn," she ordered.

He let out a big sigh. "Fine."

"You too," she shouted at me.

117

"Ugh…whatever." I crossed my arms over my chest, already fed up with this TED Talk.

"No 'whatever.' Call him. He misses you."

I grunted in acknowledgment.

"And talk to Claire," she added.

I turned my head so fast, I nearly had whiplash. "What?"

Her fists rested on her hips. "Do it. You don't have to get back together with her or anything. Just talk to her and listen to her side. I want her to resume teaching Meena ballet, and I don't want any awkwardness when she's around here."

Easy for her to say. She wasn't the one who got fucked raw and left high and dry before her dick had fully deflated.

# Chapter X

## Claire

Acold sweat broke out over the back of my neck and under my boobs as I pressed the button for the doorbell.

Three of Zayn's men formed a line behind me as I waited. He had insisted that I take more than one guard with me when I left the house and instructed me to return straight home with them.

My talk with Amelia had gone better than I'd thought it would. I had been too nervous to face her before, especially since she was Jai's family. I wouldn't have faulted her for cursing me out and never speaking to me again. I had been relieved when she gave me a chance to explain my side.

After hearing her experience at the hands of evil men like my father and brother, I felt a kinship with her. And the revelation that Jai's mother had met a similar fate to my mother had shaken me to my core.

How many women would they have to lose to realize that none of this was worth it? What price was too high for these men?

The door opened and right on cue, Shyam answered.

The words came tumbling out without any regard for syntax. "I'm here to give Meena classes…ballet…Amelia…she called me." As soon as I spit out the last word, I was ready to run away and hide from embarrassment. I didn't shy away easily, but something about Shyam always made me nervous. Kind of like a stern father figure. A broodingly handsome stern father figure, but a father figure nonetheless.

His sharp gaze examined me for a moment before sweeping to the guards behind me. Recognition flashed in his eyes. He must have already known my security detail. Holding the door open, he stepped aside, signaling for me come inside.

Zayn's men waited outside of the door as I entered.

I was greeted by a line of Shyam's own guards on either side of the door, all with eyes trained on me. My skin scorched under their scrutinizing glare.

"Follow me," Shyam ordered before striding through the entryway.

I nearly broke out into a run to keep up with his pace, and to evade close proximity to the men dressed in black behind me. They followed us through the house, never dropping their double-lined formation.

As soon as I was able to train my legs to keep up with his steps, I called out over his shoulder, "Thank you for allowing me into your home again to give Meena lessons."

The only indication I received that he had heard me was a stiff nod.

I followed him in silence the rest of the way to the private gym. The men filed in behind us, lining up on either side of the door, just like they had at the front door.

"Wait here," Shyam commanded, then turned on his heel to leave me.

"Shyam," I blurted out hastily. "Can I talk to you for a second, please?"

He glanced at his security detail before wordlessly turning back to face me, arms crossed over his chest.

"I want to apologize for keeping everything from you and your family. I'm really sorry, and I had no idea that my past would have in any way affected the safety of your family."

He continued staring, only heightening my nervousness. I cleared my throat and continued, "I really do appreciate you allowing me into your home."

"For some reason, my wife thinks that we should trust you. I have my own suspicions, but I value my wife's opinion. She's better at reading people than I am, so if she believes you, then I'll support her." His voice was quiet yet commanded attention from anyone who was near.

"But just know," he continued just as my shoulders began to relax a little, "I'll have complete surveillance when Meena has class with you. I hope you understand that, for me, this is a necessary precaution."

"I think that's completely fair." I understood and I didn't fault him for his concern. If I were him, I would have been just as cautious too. I didn't even trust Leonid, and he was my brother. How could Shyam possibly believe any words that came out of the mouth of Leonid's sister? I had, however, expected more trust from Jai.

"Madame Varon!" Meena came bursting through the door, interrupting the awkward silence that lingered. She launched her small pink-and-ruffled body into my arms. I lifted her up, hugging her tightly to me.

I had really missed my students. Teaching had been such a fulfilling part of my life. It had been the one part of my life that felt completely honest and untainted by my past.

I set her on the ground and bent over to get a good look at her face. "How have you been?"

"I missed you! Why did you stop teaching classes?" she asked.

Amelia stood behind her, greeting me with a warm smile. "Honey," she interrupted, "Madame was on vacation."

"Oh! Is that where you had your hair dyed?" Meena asked, her little forehead wrinkling with curiosity.

I giggled. "Yes."

I mouthed a silent thank-you to Amelia for saving me from having to explain my horrid story to an innocent child. No child should be privy to those horrors.

"Well, I'm glad you're back. I've been practicing my moves," Meena exclaimed, bouncing in place.

"I can't wait to see them. Should we get started?"

She nodded eagerly.

"Well, if you need us, just let us know," Amelia offered, taking her husband's arm.

Addressing the guards, her voice turned stern. "*This* will not be necessary, boys."

Shyam glared at her. "Amelia. We talked about this."

Putting on a polite yet irritated voice, she ground out. "No. You talked about it, but I never agreed." She stared Shyam down until he finally caved in.

He released a defeated sigh. "You heard her."

The men filed out of the room, their combat boots stomping on the hardwood floors in unison.

123

Amelia rose to her tiptoes, giving her husband a kiss on his cheek before they filed out of the room with their arms around each other.

Meena rolled her eyes. "Thank God those guards are gone. They creep me out!"

I chuckled, remembering how grown up she had always acted. "Shall we?" I motioned to the middle of the dance floor.

"Yeah!" she cried with glee.

\*\*\*

I hadn't realized just how much I had missed teaching until the music started and Meena and I began to move. It was evident that she had missed dance as much as I had. Any sequence that I demonstrated, she copied with attention and precision. It was the most productive class I had ever had with a student.

The time on the clock reminded me that we only had about five minutes left of class, so I decided to change the pace and switched to a variation of freestyle dancing. I explained to Meena that she would start the routine and I would follow her lead. This method of role-reversal would hone her creative-development skills.

On the sound system, I put on one of her favorite princess songs and let her take charge. She began to twirl with such gusto that she nearly fell over from the force. I followed her lead, spinning as hard as I could before landing a pose as she squealed in laughter. Meena then leapt across the room in short bursts. I mimicked her movements, making my way across the room. Meena turned around and paced through a series of spins back across the floor. I twirled on alternating legs with each revolution, until a shadow passed through the blur of my sight.

Pausing momentarily, regaining my balance, I caught a better glance. I watched the tall, tanned, figure stare at the doorhandle on the opposite side of the glass door. I could see his face clearly, and he could have seen mine if he weren't so deep in thought. The struggle going on inside of his brain read plainly across his forehead.

His hand lifted and grasped the knob. My chest pounded, hoping his internal battle led to the outcome that I desired. I wished that it were the same result that he wanted.

But my hope dissipated as I watched his hand drop back down to his side and his eyes shut tightly.

His eyes opened again, and this time, he found me with them. The yearning etched on his face was just as evident as his overbearing ego. Ultimately, his pride won out, and my heart fell into my stomach as I watched him walk away without glancing back.

I stood there pressing my hand into my abdomen, willing the clenching feeling of disappointment to subside as the soundtrack of happy love between a prince and princess grated on my ears.

The love in princess movies was a fantasy. The pain wrung through my insides was what love really felt like—messy and cruel.

# CHAPTER XI

## JAI

"What was so important that you needed to see me at nine in the morning?" I said, too distracted to greet Shyam properly as I worked the zipper of my leather jacket and removed it. The humid summer weather had left all too quickly, and in its place, the air had grown lighter and crisp, not cold enough to need a coat but chilly enough to warrant a light jacket.

"Nice to see you again, brother." That voice grabbed my attention.

Zayn sat across from Shyam, who was poised and ready for a showdown behind his desk. I should have known Shyam was up to no good when he texted me at the crack of dawn to meet him at Nirvana. His mornings were usually spent at Sethi Tech, where he took care of board issues until about lunchtime, when he ate lunch with Amelia and then relocated to Nirvana to take care of club business. I had figured that since Amelia and the kids were under lockdown, he would have been spending most of his time working remotely from home too. *Next time, I'm ignoring his damn texts.*

My jaw clenched as I narrowed in on Zayn's relaxed expression. It bothered me that he remained so composed while irritation grated my insides. I still hadn't worked up enough nerve to reach out to him like Amelia had ordered of me. But judging from his presence, Shyam had jumped again just to please his wife, leaving me to simmer in my annoyance with Zayn alone.

I tossed my jacket onto the couch across from me to free up my hands in case I needed to slap that tranquil look off his face. "What is he doing here?" I demanded.

"Come in and close the door," Shyam ordered as if I were an employee that he was prepared to have a discussion with about my failing performance and penchant for dipping into company office supplies.

"I'm not doing this." I didn't appreciate being ganged up on, especially by my own blood.

Before I could turn on my heel and storm out, Shyam called out, "Stop being a child and sit down."

I slammed the door, pissed off that despite all the shit we had been through together and how much I had helped him like a true partner, he still thought it was acceptable to speak to me like I was a kid.

I looked to the only empty chair available, conveniently positioned next to Zayn. "I'll stand," I declared, crossing my arms over my chest.

Shyam pinched the bridge of his nose. "If you want to be treated like an adult, then I'm going to need you to start acting like one. I swear, Dylan is better behaved than you, and he's a toddler."

"I refuse to sit here while you moderate like this is some bullshit intervention."

"It's not an intervention, Jai," Zayn said gently. "Sit down and let's talk this out."

I eyed him cautiously. I knew I had been holding onto this grudge for far too long, but the memory of that night when Leonid revealed Claire's identity and Zayn rushed to protect her as if she were his still infuriated me. I felt like he had turned on me and abandoned me when I needed him. Her heart wasn't the only one that had been shredded to pieces that night.

However, this talk was inevitable, even if I would rather be tortured with a rusty metal apparatus using Serbian war methods. I plopped into the open seat ready to get this over with.

"Right," Shyam started. "Leonid is still M.I.A., and his men are all still under lockdown."

"Has anyone heard from Mikhail yet?" Zayn asked.

"No. He's under lockdown too, and his every move is being monitored. We've tried to reach out to meet with him, but he hasn't answered for obvious reasons. Apparently, he helped Claire and her mother leave Russia when Leonid killed his father. He gave them new identities and ensured their safety."

I still didn't know what the fuck to call her, but Amelia kept referring to her as Claire, and Shyam seemed to be following Amelia's lead, so I guess we were now calling her by her false name.

Zayn nodded. "She told me all of this."

"Of course, she did," I said, rolling my eyes. Their closeness bothered me.

"She's fine, in case you were concerned," he shot back.

"Who the fuck asked you?" I spat.

"Maybe she would tell you if you were man enough to talk to her for one minute without losing your shit."

My hands gripped the arm rests of my chair. "Are you looking to get your ass beat?"

"Knock it off," Shyam said, slapping his desk to break up the quarrel. "We have shit to do. Leonid is still out there and is more dangerous than ever." Shyam was losing his patience with us, just like we were kids.

"Have you tracked his accounts in Lebanon?" Zayn asked.

"Everything has been cleared," I replied grimly. Connor, my accountant, had been monitoring the secret accounts Leonid had been fattening under the unsuspecting noses of his Brothers. Last night, he had called me urgently to say that all funds had been removed and he was unable to locate their trail.

"Shit," Zayn gasped. "How about his stockpile of arms?"

Shyam sighed. "Many of the warehouses we suspected he was storing them in were 'mysteriously' destroyed. No evidence of arms inside."

"He relocated those too?" Zayn asked. He had been a bit out of the loop since we hadn't been in contact with him. I felt bad that he needed to be caught up, especially since the three of us had always worked as a team.

"Yeah, but we have no intel on where they are yet," I replied. It was never good news when such a large amount of money and weapons disappeared into thin air, especially at the hands of the leader of the Bratva.

"Did our men investigate the ruins for the weapons?" Zayn asked.

"No, we had help from Le Milieu," Shyam replied.

Zayn stared in disbelief. "Le Milieu *helped* you? They don't help anyone!"

Shyam nodded. "They wanted to investigate the arms to make sure that an insider wasn't supplying Leonid."

Le Milieu, French for "The Underworld," was the mafia network in France. They dealt in various goods, but weapons were their specialty. Notoriously reclusive, Le Milieu rarely made alliances with any of the other crime organizations. They were one of the world's oldest networks, functioning since the early 1900s and still in existence today. Originally known for their prostitution industry, they later expanded to drug trafficking and robbery. Their latest and most successful endeavor was arms—the manufacturing, transporting, and selling of all things that went boom in the night.

Their base was in the French Alps, surrounded by mountains and snow, making it difficult for intruders to access them. If you could survive the trek, then you deserved the title as a worthy adversary to Le Milieu. Otherwise, they kept to themselves except when sending out shipments of arms, and it was best that the rest of the underworld gave them their privacy.

The fact that they had shared any information with Shyam completely baffled me. It was true that they respected our business, but since they fell out of the drug-trade business in the seventies to focus solely on arms, we rarely crossed paths.

"Did Alcide give you this information?" Zayn asked.

Alcide Severin. The current leader of Le Milieu. He was about the age our father would have been if he were still alive, and his family had been in charge since the 1950s. Alcide was a respected leader with very little tolerance for bullshit, much like Shyam and me. Though I had never met him personally, I knew his word could be trusted.

"He did." Shyam was so nonchalant about the whole thing, almost as if he and Alcide were old pals who golfed together.

"How the fuck did you manage that?" I asked.

"I have my ways." He wasn't going to share. Most likely, his routes of communication were something he didn't wish for Amelia to know. He wasn't supposed to be in the business anymore, yet because of me, he had been plunged back into it.

"So, what's our next move?" Zayn asked.

"We need to meet with Mikhail," I said. I needed answers from him. I needed to know if he sold me out to Leonid.

"Are you still not willing to believe her story?" Zayn asked.

That wasn't it. As much as I wanted to believe that she was a spy or that she was as deceitful as her brother because she had kept the truth from me, I knew her story was real. I had done some thinking after Amelia ripped into Shyam and me. Shyam was right, Amelia was a good judge of character. Perhaps I had been too caught up in my own shit to pay any attention to Claire's side or take a minute to understand her torment. I hadn't been able to see anything past the red that stained my vision when Zayn rushed to her side to console her.

But even when I tried to stay away from her, I couldn't get her out of my veins. The night of the glow party had certainly proven that. One whiff of her sweet scent and I'd been a goner. All the aggression we felt toward each other had bubbled over into the most explosive night I had ever had with a woman. Our chemistry hadn't dampened. No. It was even stronger.

Amelia's lecture rang in my head. I needed to make things less awkward with her if she was going to be around my niece now. I'd tried to summon the courage to speak to her during Meena's class, but my pride had gotten the best of me. I wasn't good with apologies. Admitting I was wrong was something that didn't flow out of my mouth easily.

I shrugged. "It's not that…"

"It's your pride," Shyam interrupted, playing with his pen.

I shot him a murderous look.

Zayn sighed. "You need to talk to her, man. She's been through hell and back."

"I tried." I just couldn't summon enough courage to turn the handle to the gym door to face her. I preferred unleashing my rage on her instead because it meant that she couldn't see the heartbreak that had crippled me after I ended things so horribly. Looking weak was another thing that I didn't do well.

"What happened?" Zayn looked genuinely concerned. I missed having him around.

"He chickened out," Shyam said, smirking. I made a mental note to kick his ass later.

"Shut up!" I barked at him. Letting out a huge breath, I turned toward Zayn. "I fucked up."

He nodded. "Yes, you did. So, now how are you going to fix it?"

"I dunno. It's not an easy situation."

"Imagine how it feels for her," he prodded, but his voice remained soft and encouraging.

"That's the part that guts me and keeps me from talking to her. What if I apologize and she hands me my ass?" My damn ego would be bruised.

"Then you'll have deserved it," Zayn said. "But if she still means anything to you, you need to try."

Shyam interrupted, "You'll have lots of time to do so at Meena's birthday party on Saturday."

I did a double take. "What? She's coming?"

"Don't look at me. Talk to your sister-in-law," he said.

"And you're okay with this?" I stared at him in disbelief.

Shyam shrugged.

"Just the other day, you put your wife in a headlock because she went to meet with her, and now Claire is teaching class in your home and coming to birthday parties?!"

"What?! A headlock?" Zayn glared at Shyam.

"It wasn't a headlock…and I was just trying to prove a point," he answered defensively.

"So, you're just back to normal with *her*?" I said, my sarcasm too evident to ignore.

"I don't know if my relationship with her was ever *normal*. But yeah, we talked it out," Shyam replied nonchalantly.

Zayn and I stared at him with our mouths open. "You talked? *You*, Mr. One-Word-Answer, talked something out with someone who wasn't your wife?" I asked, refusing to believe what he had just said.

"Give me a little more credit than that. I'm not a complete asshole." His lips pressed into a tight line, clearly annoyed by our doubt.

I scoffed. "What did Amelia do in bed to sway you?"

"Watch it," he snapped harshly. "That's my wife."

"Yeah, and we all know you're pussy-whipped," Zayn teased.

I chuckled. "Good one!"

Shyam rolled his eyes. "Whatever, at least I get pussy."

He might have been referring to me, but pussy wasn't my problem. I missed having my partner. Owning her heart and soul.

Zayn turned to me. "So, if I bring Claire to Meena's party on Saturday, will you act like a big boy and talk to her?"

I flashed him a look of displeasure.

"I'm serious, Jai. You can't be screaming at each other while the kid is opening birthday presents! Or fucking each other like animals in the coat closet."

So, Zayn did know what we'd been doing at the party. I grinned in satisfaction.

Shyam's brows narrowed expecting me to elaborate. Instead, I ignored him.

"Relax, Dad. I'll behave. You need to lecture her to keep her temper in check." I wasn't the only one who had the potential to cause a scene at the party. If Claire didn't provoke me, then I didn't see any problem with me keeping myself in check. Also, she needed to cover her curves up because I couldn't promise keeping her out of the coat closet if she dressed like she had at the glow party.

Zayn turned serious. "Do you promise not to chop my head off when I bring her?"

"I promise," I ground out. I hated that she lived with him, like she felt safer with him than with me. And it was all due to my bullheadedness.

I still had one nagging thing on my mind that I couldn't shake. "I need to know something," my tone lowering. "Did you sleep with her?" I held my breath waiting for his answer, knowing that I couldn't move on with my brother if his answer was what I had been dreading.

"I would never do that to you," he said gently. His face was fully relaxed and features soft.

I believed him.

"Are we still brothers?" he asked.

My lips pressed tightly with regret. I was sorry I had ever caused him to question our relationship. "Always."

# CHAPTER XII

## CLAIRE

I couldn't get the damn blouse to fall properly. The ruffles running down the bust seams were too fluffy for my liking, and I tried to smooth them down to keep from being too ostentatious.

I wasn't used to the style of clothes that the concierge had purchased for me upon Zayn's request. They had purchased a few more pieces for me since my stay with him was turning into a longer-term situation than either of us had planned for.

The loungewear they'd sent up was comfortable since they were looser fitting, but the "going out" pieces weren't what I was used to. More blouses, wrap dresses, and pencil skirts—the types of things you'd wear to "do lunch," as if I had ever been the kind of person who "did lunch."

I stared at myself in the mirror in my baby-pink, long-sleeved blouse and fitted jeans. They included a few pairs of jeggings in the shopping bags, which I was incredibly grateful for, I wished they fit a little looser.

I hadn't danced much in the past few weeks and my body had grown slightly more supple from the lack of exercise. The wall of muscle that had sheathed my core from years of dance had softened as a result, leaving a small mound of flesh available for the top button of my ultra-slim jeans to embed itself into. I figured I could just unbutton my pants under the hem of my blouse once cake was passed out. No one would know.

I had almost turned down Amelia's invite to Meena's birthday party. Jai's mood swings had me on edge, and I didn't want to be on the receiving end of his unpredictability. One day he was losing his shit on me, and the next, he was acting too awkward to even talk to me.

I had thought for sure he'd come into the gym during Meena's lesson, but whether to talk to me like a human being or unleash another bomb of disdain, I couldn't have said. But instead, he had walked away without turning back. Was it even worse that he couldn't even stand to be in the same room as me now?

Maybe he'd reached a point of apathy and would completely ignore me tonight. How had we come to this?

Even Shyam had been courteous enough to tell me how he felt. I respected his need to protect his family and didn't fault him for it. Our relationship was more like that of acquaintances. I admired his wife, and adored his children, but he and I didn't really have a strong connection where we openly discussed our lives and feelings together. I couldn't imagine that he'd have done that with many other people, except for Amelia.

But still, I was thankful that he had opened his home to me and trusted me with his daughter. It spoke volumes of the kind of man he was, unlike his hard-headed brother, who barely spoke to me anymore.

Out of respect for Amelia, I would just be polite to Jai at the party. I could muster up enough strength to say hello, then shrink into the background until Zayn said it was time to go home.

This was a special moment for the Sethi family, and Jai was still Meena's uncle. He deserved to be in the foreground at his niece's party and not have to deal with any of our shared baggage. I would just be there to extend my best wishes and support to little Meena.

The knock on the door was my alarm that it was time to go. "Come in!"

Zayn stepped in and leaned against the doorjamb. He looked effortlessly handsome in a charcoal-gray t-shirt and jeans, which was completely on-brand for him.

Unlike his brothers, he was rarely dressed up, opting for comfort over style. Shyam had the most formidable style, usually dressed in suits and dress shirts. Jai preferred graphic tees with jackets and well-fitted jeans or sometimes suits, but his style still read "expensive." I could tell that Zayn didn't care about labels which made him even more attractive.

"Ready to go?"

"Yeah, one sec." I shrugged on a wine-colored suede blazer to prepare for the chilly air outside. I guess Zayn didn't need a jacket since he was so muscular. He probably ran hot in this weather.

I grabbed Meena's present off my bed. Lana had went shopping for a present for me to give. She had taken photos of the spread in the toy aisle and sent them to me so I could pick something out and had even wrapped it in ballerina wrapping paper for me before dropping it off yesterday.

Zayn took the gift from me, and we headed on our way.

Amelia and Shyam's house was only ten minutes away from the hotel, but we rode in a blacked-out SUV with full security detail. With Leonid still on the loose, we couldn't risk walking in broad daylight where anyone of his men could easily spot us.

We made it up the stairs to the town home, with two guards following behind. I reached out to press the doorbell as Zayn stood beside me with Meena's gift tucked under his arm.

Amelia answered the door with a huge smile on her face. "Hey, guys!"

She pulled me into a tight hug. "I'm so glad you came!" she said, releasing me.

"Thanks for the invitation," I replied, grinning back at her.

"You're always welcomed here." She looked so trendy in her white jeans and vintage Chewbacca tee. I loved how down to earth she was even though she probably had millions of dollars in the bank. She still dressed like a girl you could grab some beers with.

She moved to Zayn, tucking into his huge frame. He kissed the top of her head affectionately.

"Where's the birthday girl?" he asked as Amelia moved aside to let us in.

"Running around, hopped up on sugar."

He smiled. "Nice!"

The security detail stayed outside as we followed Amelia into the house.

"Oh, I'll take that," Amelia said, grabbing my gift from under Zayn's arm.

"I didn't know what to get the little one, so I opted for money," Zayn said, handing over a fat envelope to Amelia.

She weighed the thick envelope in her hand. "Are you sure you didn't give her enough for her college tuition?"

"Money is *always* welcome as a gift in this house," Shyam said, strolling up to us in the entryway.

143

"Hey, brother," Zayn greeted him with a bro-hug, patting his back when their chests made contact.

"Hello, Claire." Shyam turned to me when Zayn pulled away. Before I could respond, he pulled me into the most awkward hug, keeping the length of his body a full foot away from me. Only his arm wrapped around my shoulders for a second, taking me by surprise.

I did my best to hide any evidence of embarrassment. "Oh...hi."

He quickly pulled away and took his place next to his wife, whose face was beaming with a bright smile. Her admiration for her husband shined so brilliantly. He kissed her cheek and took the present from her. "Let's get a drink," he said to Zayn.

I hung my jacket on the coatrack by the door and headed into the house.

Everyone filed into the spacious living room. The posh décor was now adorned with all things pink and gold. Balloons, streamers, and giant cutouts of ballerinas filled the space. To my surprise, there were more people in attendance than just family.

Amelia must have noticed my hesitation. "Meena insisted on having some of her ballet and school friends over. We didn't feel comfortable inviting everyone we knew because of..." She looked around to see if anyone could overhear before continuing, "...the current situation. So, we just opted for a few."

I couldn't see any visible security around. "Are the guards here?"

She nodded. "Not in the party space, but they're scattered around the house, watching everything."

It was probably the best option, so the other parents didn't wonder why this place was sealed like some government building.

As she excused herself to tend to some of her guests, my eyes caught the source of the background chorus of laughter and squeals. Meena was running around the room with a few of her friends I recognized from ballet class. She was the cutest thing dressed in a pink leotard and tutu, keeping with the theme of her party.

Dylan was chasing the girls but was barely able to keep up because he was much smaller than them. He spotted Zayn from the side. "Uncle Zayn!" he cried before flinging his tiny body into Zayn's thick legs. Zayn hoisted him up, tossing him into the air and then catching him in his arms. Dylan loved the wildness and shrieked his enjoyment.

My eye caught Jai talking to an older lady with red hair. She looked to be in her early sixties, but the smile on her face made her look years younger.

Impatient to get the awkwardness out of the way, I moved closer to them, waiting for him to be alone so I could say hello and relax a little more for the rest of the party.

145

To my luck, the woman spotted me and motioned for me to join them. I guess it was time to rip off the bandage.

I shuffled closer to them, offering a generic wave not intended for anyone specifically. "Hi."

Jai remained quiet, but his gaze never left me.

The older woman extended her hand. "Hello. I'm Angela, Amelia's mother."

I had thought she looked familiar. She looked exactly like her daughter, just older. They both had the same warm disposition. "I'm Claire," I said, taking her hand.

"Claire! I've heard so much about you from Amelia." She pulled me into a tight hug. "Amelia said you were beautiful, but I didn't think you would be this gorgeous," she exclaimed as she stepped back to get a better look.

Heat flushed my cheeks. "You're too kind."

"Jai! Isn't she something?" she coaxed.

His eyes raked over my body, starting from my legs, moving up my chest, and finally homing in on my hair. "The most beautiful woman in the room," he said in his low voice, dripping with heat. Oh, so *this* Jai had come to play today.

"If you'll excuse me, it looks like my daughter needs my help with something." Angela left us to help Amelia.

Nervous, I turned back to the only guy who could still make my insides jittery, even when we weren't getting along.

146

"Hello, Claire." Goosebumps spread over my chest at how smoothly my adopted name slid off his tongue. Catching me off guard, he leaned in and planted a soft kiss on my cheek. His lips lingered on my skin, the plumpness of them warming me on contact. I took a deep breath in, inhaling his intoxicating blend of spice and dominance. All too soon, he pulled away, grazing me with the scruff on his jaw.

"Hey," was all I could manage to say as I tried to catch my breath.

He reached out and took a tendril of my hair between his fingers. "I like this."

"Thanks," I said softly. He hadn't gotten to see my close-to-natural hair color at the glow party since it had been too dark, and he must have been too distracted to notice it inside the gym. But now, he studied the hue as if he were trying to memorize it.

"What prompted this change?" he asked.

"Nothing really. Just no longer have a reason to be an unnatural blonde."

His fingers stilled as the rest of his body stiffened. It was as if he had just been reminded of the reason we weren't together all over again—and why I had to change my hair in the first place.

Saving me from further unease like the guardian angel he was, Zayn appeared, pulling Jai into another bro-hug. And judg-

147

ing from their embrace, they seemed to be back on good terms now. At least one relationship had been salvaged in this mess.

As I turned away to give them their space, a hand grabbed mine. I turned back to see who it belonged to, though I already knew from his touch. "Don't go too far," Jai said quietly just so I could hear.

I walked away, desperate for a moment to cool off from all the heat he emanated. The snack table seemed safe enough. The shiny gold bowls holding an array of treats were my reprieve from Jai's gravitational pull. After scooping out a small helping onto a white plate with a border of ballet shoes around the edge, I lingered near the table.

My solitude was interrupted by a few familiar faces—parents of one of my former ballet students, Isabelle.

"How come you're not teaching anymore?" Isabelle's mother asked. She looked a lot like her daughter, with long black hair and olive-colored skin.

I didn't really have an answer prepared since I hadn't been expecting to run into anyone from my ballet life. She obviously hadn't heard of the 'family emergency' excuse that Zayn had used to get me out of teaching indefinitely, so I kept my reply general. "Um…just on a brief hiatus."

Isabelle's father was just as good looking with his dark brown hair. "Well, whenever you come back, please do let us know.

You were Isabelle's favorite teacher at the school. She keeps saying she wants to be a ballerina when she grows up."

I blushed. The feeling that I had affected a child's life warmed me inside. "That's really amazing. I will definitely let you know when I return." I was hoping that would happen one day, but realistically, it might never happen. Would I always be in hiding from Leonid?

"Have you ever thought of opening up your own school?" the mother asked.

"Maybe one day, but far in the future." Although my initial passion had been performing, teaching had become a part of me. Having a chance to encourage younger generations meant a lot to me.

"Sign us up!" they said in unison.

More parents of former students found us and engaged me in small talk about dance and their girls. It was nice to be around other people for a change.

After some time, Amelia motioned for everyone to gather around the completely decked-out dining table. We all huddled around with a clear view of the balloon banner on the wall behind it.

Amelia set the pink sprinkle-covered cake down on the gold tablecloth, and Angela set about lighting the candles.

"Where's Meena?" Amelia shouted, looking over the crowd of heads to find the birthday girl.

"Here she is!" Jai appeared from behind the crowd with Meena perched on his shoulders. Zayn joined in, carrying Dylan on his hip, while Shyam filed in next to Amelia.

Jai lifted Meena off his shoulders and set her down on the chair in front of the cake. Her eyes flared wide with excitement at the mounds of frosting.

We all sang "Happy Birthday" off-key as Dylan clapped along gleefully. When it was time to blow out the candles, Meena shut her eyes so tightly that her entire face wrinkled up. Then she let out a huge puff, extinguishing the sparkly candles. We all clapped in celebration.

Shyam grabbed the cake knife on the table and cut a slice out for Meena, then fed a bite to her. Her face lit up with the first taste of sugary goodness. Jai whispered into her ear, causing her smile to widen even further. She took the fork from her father and shoved it into the slice, drawing out a large bite and then offering it to Shyam. He leaned in to accept it, but at the last second, Meena smashed the piece into his nose, leaving a giant smudge of frosting across it.

The entire party broke out in laughter. Shyam grabbed a glob of cake and flung it at Jai, hitting the side of his face. Everyone died from the hilarity of the scene that played out.

The entire Sethi family, including Jai, Angela, and Zayn, posed as a professional photographer, along with the rest of us using our phones, snapped photos.

Adoration filled Amelia's eyes as she wrapped her arms around her husband and looked up at him. The shutter of the camera went wild as the photographer moved in to capture the moment. Shyam leaned down and kissed her on the lips.

As I moved my camera to capture the loving couple in frame, snapping away, my eye caught Jai watching them embrace from the side. A smile was plastered onto his lips, but his eyes couldn't hide the longing and hint of sadness that lived in them. Not too long ago, that had been us, holding each other and showering one another with love. *Jai, I miss it too.*

After we all had our fill of cake, we moved to the living room so Meena could open her presents. Amelia tried to insist she wait until later, after everyone left, but Shyam caved to his daughter's wishes and suggested she just open a few now to celebrate.

She ripped into each gift with gusto, sending shreds of wrapping paper flying through the air like heavy snow. Every time a gift was finally revealed, she would wave it in the air while screaming with excitement. Amelia struggled to keep up as she recorded the name of each donor in a small notebook while we all gushed over the gifts Meena showed us.

"Oh, my goodness! I've always wanted a Barbie Ballerina Studio," the birthday girl exclaimed as she investigated the contents through the clear window of the packaging.

"Who gave you that one, Meena?" Amelia asked, ready to scribble the name down in her book.

Meena searched the room as if she were looking for someone to speak up.

"I did," I offered.

Meena jumped up from the floor and ran over to me, throwing her arms around my neck. As if that weren't precious enough, she pressed a rough kiss to my cheek in gratitude. I squeezed her back.

"Thank you, Madame Varon! I really love my present."

"You are so welcome, sweetie." As she pulled away from me to run back to her spot on the floor to attack more gifts, I caught Jai staring at me. Warmth filled his dark eyes and a soft smile spread over his lips. He was a beautiful man when he was genuinely happy like this.

I couldn't help but return the sentiment with a smile of my own. Although things weren't like what they used to be before Leonid came to New York, this dynamic between us was way more comfortable than the fighting we had done in recent weeks. I would forever miss the passion we had shared, but I could tolerate these pleasantries.

Just as the sun set, turning the sky into a pinkish-purple hue, guests started to say their goodbyes and head out. Exhausted children, crashing after the high of sugar and fun, were carried out one by one in their parents' arms, in addition to an overfilled goody bag as a parting gift.

Seeing as my ride was Zayn, who had disappeared with Jai and Shyam somewhere, I couldn't exactly leave just yet. Amelia, Angela, and the maid were busy clearing the mess left behind and restoring the house to its original pristine condition.

I followed suit and grabbed an empty garbage bag to clear up the living room where bits of wrapping paper still littered the silk rug and pink cups cluttered the accent tables. The adults were obviously tidier than the children, who had left their dishes everywhere. I started in the far corner of the room, tossing trash into the bag.

A dark shadow in my periphery distracted my attention from my task. Jai stood there looking delicious in his jeans and signature graphic tee, which clung to the curves of his firm pecs. Even if I hadn't slept with him in the past, it would have been difficult to ignore his physique. He was a good-looking man, and I just happened to know what was hiding underneath his clothes.

His strides were slow and smooth, as if to keep his prey, me, from running away. Wordlessly, he took the bag from my hand and held it open.

I smiled shyly. "Thanks." I continued to pick up trash and deposit it as he watched over me, but the building pressure in the silence overwhelmed me.

153

Attempting to break the tension, I spoke. "It was a nice party."

He simply nodded in response.

I continued, "Meena seemed happy with how it turned out."

The mention of his niece broke his silence. "I can't believe she's six."

"She's a big girl now."

He shook his head in amazement. "It's crazy. I still see her as a baby. A bossy one, but still a baby."

I chuckled.

Jai set the bag off to the side. Staring intently into my eyes, he neared me. "That's a nice sound," he hummed, his eyes glazed over with a dreamy expression.

I knew that look well. I had seen it every time he gazed into my eyes after a night filled with love making. After he came inside of me, he would always have the same look he had now, one that let me know I was the only woman who occupied his thoughts.

"Jai," I breathed out.

He inched closer to me, until he was less than an arm's length away. "I'm sorry, Claire. I was an ass." He rubbed the back of his neck sheepishly. "Everything I said that night…you didn't deserve any of it."

The shock of his apology robbed me of breath. I hadn't been expecting any remorse from him, especially today. As much as I wanted to accept it in this moment, I had heard similar words from him before, and his explosive temper formed a pattern that I had been on the receiving end of one too many times.

He sensed my hesitation. "You don't have to accept it. I just wanted to say it, so you would know how I felt."

"Why are you saying this now?" I whispered.

"I've been doing some thinking lately."

I nodded. "Thinking is good."

"Do you mind if I stop by tomorrow to talk?" He looked around for any sign of an audience. "I don't want to do it here."

I shrugged. "Sure. I'm free as a bird." Oddly enough, I was about as free as a caged bird, but the expression had just tumbled out of me to disguise my anxiety.

His smile of appreciation reached his eyes, highlighting the twinkle inside of them and making me forget my trepidation.

Closing the distance between us, he reached out and placed his fingers under my chin, tipping my face up to look at him. He pressed a soft kiss against my cheek. My breath no longer existed in that moment. He slowly pulled back, until his lips were just in front of mine, not quite touching.

"Goodnight, Claire," he murmured, making my lips tingle with his warm breath. No teasing. No aggression. Just pure longing.

"Good night," I whispered.

# Chapter XIII

## Jai

W aiting for Zayn to answer my knock was a surreal experience. I felt like a teenage boy asking to see his daughter—too weird for me.

Even though I had a copy of the keycard to his suite, I had thought it would have been inappropriate to use it since we were still working on our relationship. So instead, I had rapped on the door like a common door-to-door salesman.

The door opened, revealing Zayn's mammoth frame hogging the entire doorway. "Hey. What's up?"

"I came to talk to Claire. Is she in?" Of course, she was. Where else would she have been? She had been a prisoner since the day she was born.

"Yeah, sure. Come in."

I followed him into the suite with my hands tucked into my jean pockets. "Want a scotch?" he asked.

"Nah, I should probably stay sober for this." Lately, my temper had been looking for any excuse to rear its ugly head.

"Good idea," he agreed. "Coffee?"

"Sounds good."

"Want a latte?" he asked innocently.

"What the fuck, man? That's basically coffee-flavored milk. I'll take an espresso." What was the point of coffee if you needed to drown it in milk? I wanted to taste that smooth bitterness as the coffee made its way down, burning my insides.

I took a seat on one of the barstools tucked under the kitchen island as Zayn set to work on the high-tech, instant-espresso maker on the counter. He placed a foil pod into the top of the machine and pressed the start button. Espresso shot into a clear glass, the creamy foam settling at the top like a chocolate-colored cloud.

When it was done, I took the glass from Zayn and threw it back like it were a shot of tequila, feeling the heat scald the back of my throat in a pleasurable way.

He took the seat next to me. "You two seemed civil yesterday," he said, before sipping the nearly white latte he had made for himself.

"Yeah," I replied, fiddling with my empty cup. I hadn't been sure that we could keep the peace for the duration of the party, but it had turned out better than I could have imagined. I had even gotten the chance to apologize. To be honest, I hadn't said it hoping she'd accept it. I had owed her that apology, and she'd needed to hear the words.

Zayn cradled his cup in his hands between is knees on the barstool. "She seems nervous today. Must have sensed you were coming."

"Yeah, I asked her if it would be okay to stop by, and she said 'yes'."

"She was jumpy this morning for breakfast. Knocked her plate over. Eggs went flying everywhere." He grinned, shooting me a sidelong glance.

"No way!" I chuckled at the visual. She had always been cute when she was nervous. It made me happy knowing I still had that effect on her.

"Yeah, and then she crawled on her hands and knees to clean it up, blaming it on being distracted by some choreography she was planning for Meena."

"She really doesn't like to admit when anyone ruffles her feathers, does she?"

"She's one hell of a woman, that's for sure," Zayn said.

She really was perfect. Any guy would be lucky to have her. She was the type that turned heads in a room, not just because of her insane beauty, but because of her grace and confidence.

Any man would be an idiot to pass up the chance to claim her in bed.

My gut churned thinking of another man touching her. Kissing her. Making love to her.

"I have to ask again," I started, keeping my voice low. "Were you ever attracted to her while she's been staying with you?"

"She's a pretty girl," he said as he shook his head. "But she's not my type." His answer was earnest. I had never known him to tell a lie.

"Why not?" She was fucking gorgeous, and he was a red-blooded man. Why wouldn't he be attracted to her?

He stared me dead in the eye. "Because...her heart belongs to *you*."

I felt like more of a dick than ever for thinking they had hooked up after our breakup. I was a moron for thinking that Zayn would have done that to me. "I'm so sorry for accusing you of shit, man. I now realize that you'd never betray me like that. I just couldn't see straight through all of my frustration."

"I get it. You were hurt. People do shitty things when they're hurt."

I had never heard truer words. My mind was the fucking devil's playground when I was alone with my thoughts, reaching for any destructive answer to warrant my misery.

"I'd never do that to you or Shyam. But I'm not into women like her, anyway."

"*Who* is your type?" I had never really seen him with anyone. Sure, he'd get the occasional lap dance at the strip club, but I had never actually seen him hook up with a woman. His love life was a mystery to me.

"Don't worry about it," he answered dismissively.

My eyebrow hitched high with even more interest now that he was being so secretive.

Before I could probe further, that familiar French accent perfumed my ears with pleasure. "Hey."

Zayn and I both turned to see her standing in front of us in a navy-blue wrap dress and bare feet. I could tell the overly mature clothes she wore weren't of her own choosing, but I guess she didn't have much of a choice with not having access to her own possessions anymore. "Hey."

Zayn stood up as if on cue. "Well, I have some errands to run. I'm leaving some of my men behind as backup security." He patted me on the shoulder before heading out the door. "I'll catch up with you guys in a bit."

The poor guy was always leaving the room so we could talk.

Claire remained glued to the spot with her arms folded over her chest and her discomfort as bright as a beacon. I was just as nervous, but better at hiding it.

I motioned to Zayn's now vacated seat. "Do you want to sit down?"

161

"Sure," she replied quietly. She perched on the edge with her body facing mine.

More silence.

For two people who had had a hell of a lot happen between them, words were things that didn't flow as easily as they should have.

I bit the bullet. "How have you been?"

She shrugged. "Stressed, I guess."

"We'll find Leonid," I reassured her.

She didn't believe me, and I couldn't blame her. "You can't be sure of that."

"I'm confident in the ability of my men."

"And then what will you do?"

Not understanding her meaning, I tilted my head to the side. "What do you mean?"

"Once you capture Leonid. What will you do to him?" she pressed.

"You should already know the answer to that."

As if caught off guard by my response, her shoulders stiffened.

Maybe she had been expecting me to show him mercy, but there was no way I could let him walk free. "Come on. You know this is how we handle *problems* in this world."

"I just never thought *you* would be part of it. The guy I... the guy I used to love. I don't care how painful Leonid's death is. But hearing you talk about killing people isn't something I can get used to." Her once bright blue eyes now seemed grayer, clouded with the storms crashing inside of her.

"Claire, I can't change that." This was what I did for a living—pay retribution to those who dared to defy me.

"I know." She grimaced. "Do you enjoy it?"

"Enjoy killing people?" I clarified.

She waved her hand in the air jerkily. "All the death. The bad men. The lies."

"Honestly, it's all I've ever known." I never thought that I'd be the one to rule over the empire, but I certainly knew that I would support Shyam as he grew our business.

"I understand that. From the time I was a child, I knew that I would never leave this world. I would be used as a pawn, just like my mother was, and married off to the whatever monster would bring fortune and power to my father—or, rather, Leonid." It was clear that her brother wanted to marry her off to the highest bidder just to fatten his pockets.

"And that's why Leonid fought so hard to find you?"

"It definitely is. He even said it himself. I've been gone for over five years. My absence didn't ruin his tyranny, but my presence would certainly strengthen it." Her shoulders drooped hopelessly.

The idea of her married off to some devil who would treat her like property sickened me. Men in our world didn't treat

163

their wives with respect. Women were property to be molded to the liking of the men that owned them. Claire had so much more fire and intelligence than to settle for a life like that. She needed to be pursuing her passions and building a legacy of her own. "It'll never come to that."

"I hope you're right." Her weak smile faded. "But I'm not so sure you realize how devious Leonid is. He'll stop at nothing to get what he wants."

I lifted my hand as if taking an oath. "I swear on my life that you will never be used for the benefit of the Bratva."

She held my gaze. "So does this mean you don't believe that I'm a spy?"

I wanted to believe the worst of her. I had convinced myself that she deserved punishment because she had betrayed me more than by breaking my heart. She was the sister of my enemy. I'd needed another reason to plunge the knife embedded in my heart back into hers. I'd needed to believe that she had tricked me in order to go on; otherwise, the heartbreak would have killed me. The desire for vengeance was the only thing that held me together.

But I knew my theory was wrong.

"I think, deep down, I never believed you were," I admitted.

"Then why did you say all of those heinous things to me? You called me 'a lying Russian whore.'" Her eyes glistened as she recalled the poison I'd spewed at her.

My hands flew to her face, cradling it gently as I made her focus on my eyes. "You don't know how badly I regret those words. If I could take them back, I would. I was blindsided by the truth about your past. And the fact that Leonid, the person I hate most in this world, was the one to reveal it ripped me."

Tears were now streaming down her face. I stroked my thumbs through the little rivers born of heartache and sorrow because of my rage. "I was scared for my life. I didn't know who I could trust. You were the first person I had ever wanted to confide in."

"I'm so sorry that I didn't listen to your side after Leonid revealed everything. What can I say to make you stop crying?"

"Nothing!" Fire suddenly roiling behind her tears, she pushed my hands away and pounded on my chest as hard as she could, while she sobbed. "I hate you. I hate you for not telling me about what you really did for a living. I hate you for doing business with Leonid!" Her voice grew louder, and her punches grew stronger with every sentence she unleashed. I let her take her anger out on me. It was the least I could do for all the shit I had put her through.

When she was too overwhelmed to continue hitting me, she collapsed into my arms, her face burrowed into my chest as she cried. With one hand stroking her hair and the other on her back, I could feel each heaving tremor as her sobs tore through her.

165

"Baby girl, forgive me." It was the first time I had used my special name for her since we broke up, but somehow, it just felt right.

She pulled back, as stunned by the endearment as I had been when it slipped off my tongue. I waited for her to argue or ban me from using that name ever again. Instead, she remained silent, staring at me with wonder through her wet eyes as I spoke. "I know I don't deserve your trust, but I'll do anything to get it back."

She continued to stare at me, her expression unreadable. My gut vibrated with anticipation.

Her eyes narrowed in on my mouth, desperation to narrow the gap between us evident all over her face. But I wasn't going to do it. It was up to her to take what she wanted, not the other way around.

"Tell me what you want, Claire." The attraction between us had never faded. In fact, it felt stronger than ever before. I knew she felt it too.

"Kiss me," she begged.

I shook my head. "No."

Confusion wrinkled her forehead.

"You've spent your whole life having men like me take from you. It's time for you to take what you want."

Realization of my intent dawned on her. For once, she had a choice. She could walk away and never forgive me. Or she

166

could have me in this moment, the way that I longed to have her.

Her mouth crashed into mine, bruising my lips with its intensity. Strawberry lip balm and salty tears fused together perfectly to describe this moment—sensual and overwhelming.

I accepted whatever she gave, grateful to be able to taste her again. When her tongue dipped into my mouth, I welcomed it with mine, tangling in a wet embrace.

She moved from her seat to straddle my lap, her hands weaving through my hair as we lost ourselves. Tilting her head to deepen the angle at which she could consume my mouth, she gripped my scalp with her fingers. Our kiss grew more desperate and frenzied, as we couldn't satisfy our fill of each other.

"Wrap your legs around me," I ordered. As I scooped my hands under her ass, she obliged. I sucked at her bottom lip as I walked her down the hall. I had been to Zayn's suite before so I knew where the guestroom was.

I kicked the door shut once we were inside. Together, we tumbled onto the bed in a tangle of arms and legs.

Her hands pulled at the neckline of my t-shirt, unsuccessfully trying to remove it. Coming to her aid, I shed the cloth, tossing it aside and exposing my chest for her wandering hands to explore.

My mouth delved into the crook of her neck, tasting her natural sweetness. Her intoxicating moans urged me to keep going, licking down to the valley of her breasts. The dress she wore might not have been true to her style, but it sure as hell worked in my favor with how much cleavage it revealed when tugged the right way. As I pulled on the fabric at her chest, it fell open, still held together at her waist, exposing her heavenly, lace-clad tits. Thank God she wasn't wearing another damn leotard, sealed shut like a straitjacket.

Unable to hide my excitement, I chuckled.

"What's so funny?"

"Nothing. It's just that this might be the most accessible outfit you've ever worn."

Her swollen lips parted to let out a fit of giggles, that lit up her whole face. If I could have, I would have recorded that laugh and stored it in my mind just to play on a whim. It was the most beautiful sound that my ears had ever heard.

My attention quickly shifted back to the feast before me. Her breasts spilled over the cups of her bra. The piece of clothing seemed to be too small to contain her mounds. Normally, they were perfect handfuls of flesh, but in that tight excuse for underwear, they were bursting out of the seams that failed to contain them.

Pushing the cups down and holding one plump mound in place, I feasted on her hard peak. Licking. Sucking. Biting. I teased the smooth, dark pink flesh, making her back arch into my touch. The half-moan-half-pants coming from her throat sounded more animal than human.

I pulled on the sash around her waist, and the dress fell completely open, revealing the rest of her forbidden fruit. My hands clutched her breasts as I sprinkled kisses down her belly. Her abs had always been tight and hard, but the lack of exercise had made the area grow softer and more supple. I had loved her physique before, but I loved what I saw now even more.

I sucked hard at the lower part of her waist, right above her hip, causing her to cry out from the sharp pain. Releasing her skin, I smiled with pride at the mark I had left on her belly. My mark.

"You're evil," she purred, grinning at my satisfaction. Honey strands splayed on the bed around her like a halo.

"I can't help that I find you so sexy that I need to claim any skin I touch."

With her hand propped softly against the side of her head, she captured her lower lip between her teeth.

My cock jerked painfully as I imagined him pushing his way between those full lips, lightly grazing her teeth on the way in.

My eyes trained on her, I pulled down her matching lace panties. I would get my turn another time; today was about her. Today was about me making it up to her for as long as she would have me.

169

I pressed kisses to the smattering of dark hair. The color looked similar to the hair on top of her head. As a guy drunk off her pussy, I had never questioned the difference in hues, but now, I understood it all.

Her moan rang out, humming through my ears as I pulled her nub between my lips. The tip of my tongue stroked her sensitive area, sending her twisting under my touch. My hands weaved around the backs of her legs and held onto her inner thighs, controlling the distance between them. I was ready to consume what I had been missing for far too long. I lapped at her folds like a starved fool who had once stupidly turned her offering away.

The scent of her enthusiasm was my motivation. The taste of her arousal was my fuel. The erratic flicks of her hips against my face, begging for more, were my purpose. I would die a happy man if this were the last task I completed on Earth.

"Baby girl, you're the sweetest thing I've ever tasted," I groaned against her pussy, her wetness coating the hairs on my chin.

"Jai, I missed you."

"I fucking missed you too." How the hell had I gone this long without tasting her? *Stupid man.*

I slid my hands up higher to her ass cheeks, kneading them with my fingers as my mouth buried into her sex. Parting the flesh, I tilted her hips up to present her lower hole to me. In one long stroke, I slid my tongue down, swiping around the puckered flesh before pushing through the resistance.

Her hips jerked, startled by the new intimacy. "Jai, what are you..."

Before she could contest, I moved back to her pussy to relax her. She was anything but silent with the moans she hummed out, but at least she wasn't arguing.

My tongue worked her clit as I slid two fingers into her wet pussy, milking her. Sticky, warm fluid coated my fingers. It would be enough for what I had planned for her. Withdrawing my digits with force, I left her whimpering at the loss of the filling sensation in her depths.

Smearing her silken honey between my fingers, I glazed my thumb with sweetness. "Angle your hips up a little more for me, angel."

She stared down at me with skepticism, as if I were a magician full of tricks. But I was—I had tricks that would have her eyes rolling back into her pretty little head.

Slowly, she tilted upward, giving me more access to her ass. I pressed on her thighs to widen them, completely exposing both holes to me.

Sealing my mouth over her pussy once again, I worked her with my tongue, bringing her close to her threshold. Her sounds of pleasure guided me through my progress.

Satisfied with the depths of pleasure she had reached; I made my move. My lubricated thumb teased her asshole as I quickened the pace of my tongue. Instead of protesting like I knew she wanted to, she submitted to the sensations threatening to pull her under.

Broaching her resistance, I dipped my thumb further inside. Only the tip made it through, but the girth of my digit was large enough for her to feel the burn of bliss. She cried out, surrendering to my sneak attack. My tongue alternated between her slit and her nub, offering her a variety of sensations to overload her nerves.

Her body tensed as sweat slicked her thighs around my face. Moving my thumb in small circular motions, I felt her walls pulse against the tip of my tongue as I drank from her fountain.

In one quick move, I pushed my thumb deeper inside her rear hole as my tongue wrote messages of my feelings for her along her sex. Her body thrashed as she met her edge, exploding into a fit of elation. Her pulses of delight were so strong that they squeezed down on my thumb with each wave of ecstasy.

"*Mon dieu!*" she screamed.

Her body collapsed onto the mattress, too limp from exhaustion to move. Sitting back on my heels, I took in the sight of her completely spent due to my hard work.

She smiled lazily up at me, barely able to keep her eyes open against the sleep trying to take hold. "You're turn," she sighed with satisfaction.

Her ambition amused me. She couldn't have given more even if she tried.

Instead, I moved beside her, wrapping an arm around her waist. Pressing a kiss against her head, I whispered, "Next time."

Smiling gratefully, she drifted off into slumber while I watched her, soaking in the beauty next to me.

# CHAPTER XIV

## JAI

I t would have been nice to hold a meeting in something other than a dilapidated building or a grimy alleyway. A well-lit cigar club or a yacht on the crystal blue waters of the Mediterranean would have been a great change of pace.

Instead, men like me were forced to meet men like him in the dark of night in an abandoned factory.

I knew Mikhail had finally managed to slip away from Leonid's watch to meet me when a simple text from an unidentified number lit up my phone: *Murder*.

A nickname for Mattapan, Boston, or "Murderpan," as the locals had once called it due to its high levels of crime. I knew exactly where he meant.

It was one of our designated meeting areas with Mikhail. We had acquired several around the world over the years and rotated locations for each meeting to avoid being discovered. We would message each other using non-traceable burner phones with one-word clues for places to meet or information we had for each other.

Driving three and a half hours from Manhattan to the abandoned factory in Boston wasn't what I had expected to be doing with my evening. Lying next to Claire with my arms wrapped around her was where both my mind and heart wanted to be.

The warmth of her fully sated body against mine lingered on my skin, kindling the fire that still burned for her inside of me. Our attraction had never died during this whole sordid mess, but the feeling of her falling apart under my touch was incomparable to the lustful hate that we had engaged in just to satisfy our needs.

I traced the delicate outline of her face with my eyes over and over again to memorize every detail. After weeks apart, I felt even more protective of her now, and I was terrified of spending even a second longer without her.

She hadn't officially accepted my apology, but she knew of my remorse. I wanted to be there when she woke up to feed her more of my feelings for her and to make love to her for as long as she would have me.

But when my phone had buzzed in my pocket, I knew my time was up.

Mikhail's text had sent adrenaline coursing through my veins. I needed to get to the bottom of his fidelity to me and hear what really happened when he aided Claire and Camile's escape.

As quietly as I could, I texted Shyam in code so he would organize a car and await my arrival at his doorstep.

I took one last look at my sleeping angel and pressed a kiss to her lips before sliding out from under her. I dressed and left her room as softly as possible, locking her door from the inside since she was half-dressed. She would be safe at Zayn's place, but I didn't want anyone walking in on her and seeing what was only meant for my eyes. She was still mine, even if we hadn't discussed the future of "us" yet, and I'd have to kill any man who saw her in that state.

Zayn still hadn't returned from his "errands" by the time I left, so I sent him a quick text to say that I was heading out and that Claire was asleep. I didn't mention anything about meeting Mikhail since I was in a rush, though I probably should have told him everything. It was better that he would return home and stay with Claire while I was gone.

Much of Zayn's security had still been roaming around the suite, so I didn't deem it necessary to leave any of my men behind. My guards drove me straight over to Shyam's and I left them to watch after Amelia and the kids. We expected to be back my morning, but it was prudent that we fattened their protection, especially since we couldn't take any of the men with us for fear of being too conspicuous. Even our car would have to be one of the nondescript ones that we kept for situations like this.

The air was chilly, and the light mist of rain felt like little needles on my warm skin. Our strides were long since we were eager to get inside quickly, and every so often, puddles of water splashed under our shoes.

The large metal door was closed but always remained unlocked. The procedure was that the last of us to step inside would lock the door from the inside. After securing the lock, we continued to the rusted stairwell. The only light to guide us was that of the sparse lights shining in the alleyway outside, so we relied on memory and our hands to find our way.

Judging from the feeling under my fingers as I held the railing, its paint had long ago begun to flake off in big chunks, exposing the cold metal underneath. We descended the well until our feet landed on cement rather than metal stairs. A quick right was the only path available, based on my memory.

The hallway was narrow, and it was easy to bump into the walls if you weren't paying attention. My palm grazed the wall for guidance, feeling the unevenness of the cracked drywall. I felt for the bump in the dry wall that would indicate that we had arrived at the correct door.

My footsteps ceased, and soon, Shyam's did as well. As I pushed the door open, dim light from a desk lamp greeted us. My eyes focused on Mikhail standing in the far corner of the room as Shyam shut the door.

In his early sixties, Mikhail still looked strong and lethal. His thick, graying hair was a stark contrast to his muscular physique and tattooed skin. The younger Bratva men kept their heads shaved, but Mikhail had kept with the old customs of preserving his aging appearance.

The dark shading of a skull peeked out from the collar of his black trench coat. The man was perhaps the most eloquent of his Brothers due to his wisdom but also the worst one to have as an enemy.

His loyalties had always lain with Nicholai's father, the former *Pakhan*. But ever since Nicholai had taken over, and now Leonid, Mikhail had found it difficult to stand by and watch the subsequent *Pakhans,* in his words, "desecrate the traditions of Russia." He hated the deals that Nicholai had made, like trafficking humans, and had even worked with us to secure Amelia's safety when Nicholai threatened to take her.

As little a fan as I was of the Bratva, Mikhail had been a man of his word and honor. I was still in disbelief that he could have betrayed me for Leonid by luring me to the restaurant to set me up, but the coincidence of his text with Leonid's whereabouts followed by Claire's appearance that day was too powerful to ignore.

My eye caught on a chair opposite of Mikhail. Well-fitted leather shoes were planted firmly in front of the chair legs, but the face of their owner was hidden by the shadows cast over it.

Who the hell was this? We were never to bring *guests* unannounced to these meetings. Had Mikhail betrayed me again? Was this another trap that Leonid himself had constructed? I took the bait yet again.

My spine stiffened as I clenched my hands into fists at my sides. "You betrayed me," I seethed, my voice thick with contempt. "You set me up today just like you did at *Semya*."

I tried harder to make out the figure, thinking it might be Leonid, but the person was too tall and thin to be that son of a bitch.

Mikhail noticed what had caught my attention. He cleared his voice, most likely to signal his guest to introduce himself.

The person stood up, rising to a formidable height. Shyam and I were fairly tall men, but this person rivaled us in stature.

As he stepped into the soft glow of the light, his hard features were revealed. Sharp jaw, thin nose, high cheek bones. Thick gray hair that reminded one he was still a force to be reckoned with. His knowing smirk was that of an authority who knew strategy as well as he knew money.

"Alcide," Shyam greeted the man, unable to disguise the surprise in his voice.

I had never met Alcide Severin before. Shyam had only ever been in his company once before, but it had been years since then.

The infamous leader of Le Milieu was a recluse, only traveling outside of France when he deemed it necessary. Though he was rarely seen, the entire underworld knew his name and reputation as the father of the Underworld. Since he had been a crime lord for much longer than Shyam and I, Alcide was wise and more cunning than either of us.

I was one to give credit where it was due, and I acknowledged that Alcide had paved the way for the new age of the Sethi empire and all the other crime organizations in the world. Because we dealt different products, we had never been competitors, and our business had been allowed to grow exponentially without any retribution from Alcide.

"Gentlemen," he spoke. His fitted suit clung to his tall, lean frame. He wasn't thick and muscular like Mikhail, but I could tell his body would move quickly during combat from how lithe he seemed. "It's been far too long, Shyam. And Jai, it's wonderful to finally meet you in person."

Unable to comprehend his presence, I merely nodded at his acknowledgment of me.

"What brings you all the way out here?" Shyam asked, his gaze bouncing between Alcide and Mikhail, searching for answers.

"The same reason that you are all the way out here?" he replied, the apathy in his voice cooler than the draft in the room.

I directed my attention to Mikhail, who had been standing silently in the corner this whole time. "Where is he?"

"Back in Russia," he answered curtly. Mikhail was a direct man. It was probably why I found him to be a valuable informant.

"Why?" His business in New York was far from finished. He didn't have my head on a platter or Claire in his filthy clutches.

"He claimed he had a pressing issue with the Serbs."

A huff of a scoff escaped me. I found that explanation to be odd since the Serbs were his allies now; *they* followed his commands. I would have thought terrorizing his sister would take precedence over his minions. "And you believe him?"

"Absolutely not," he said.

"Why are you here setting me up again instead of with your *Pakhan*?" I ground out through my teeth. Mikhail was his most senior brother. Surely, he'd want him by his side when he met with his allies.

"I never set you up. I pledge allegiance to Bratva, not to Leonid. He is not Bratva in my eyes." Mikhail's gaze was intense, as if he were insulted that I had referred to Leonid as his leader. Mikhail knew as well as I did that he was not the rightful leader of the Bratva after he stole the crown away from his own father. "He took half his men. The rest of us are to stay and keep our eyes on *you*."

Shyam was still focused on Alcide. "As much as we're glad that you could join us tonight, how do Leonid's issues with the Serbs involve you, Alcide?"

"My business isn't with Leonid and his alliances. My concern lies with another Petrov."

I did a double take, making sure I understood who he was referring to. "You mean Claire?" What business could he possibly have with her?

A wry smile spread across his thin lips. "Sure. Whatever name she wishes to go by now."

With the rest of his body remaining still, Shyam's head turned to flash me a questioning glance. He was just as puzzled as I was.

Mikhail remained quiet with his hands clasped in front of him, giving Alcide the floor.

"What dealings do you have with her?" My tone was abrasive, but I didn't care. She was innocent in all of this, and

I wasn't about to let her get sucked back into this world of bad men that she had so desperately tried to avoid.

"Forgive me for my bluntness, but she is my business," Alcide said, seemingly irritated by my possessiveness.

I didn't understand how she meant anything to Le Milieu. Sure, she was Bratva royalty, but she hadn't been in contact with the brotherhood in years and had even tried to flee. She had simply been born into the wrong family at the wrong time.

"How is she?" he pressed.

"How do you know her?" I countered, heat building under my leather jacket.

Alcide ignored my question as if he were in the middle of a daydream. "Those pretty blue eyes. And that full head of hair, like light caramel. It's such a shame she had to dye it blonde to hide from her brother."

How the fuck did he know so much about her? Had he seen her? Was he stalking her too, like Leonid? Whatever the answer was, I didn't appreciate his longing tone.

Grinning as if to spur me on even further, he said, "I bet she's grown into such a beautiful woman." he grinned.

Was this motherfucker lusting after what was mine? I didn't care that he was an elder in our world—he could have been goddamn Zeus—I would have his head if he didn't shut the fuck up.

Sensing my blood boiling in my veins, Shyam grabbed my bicep to keep me in my place. I had once done the same to him when Amelia's honor was at stake in India at the hands of Tarun.

"I expect she's just as beautiful as her mother was," he continued.

I looked at Shyam, whose forehead was just as creased as mine with questions. Alcide had known her mother?

Trying to diffuse the situation, Mikhail took over. "Alcide, I sense Jai is ready to rip you to shreds over Claire. Better get to the point quickly."

"So, you care for her?" Alcide asked, his eyebrow hitching as if only expecting one answer.

"Care" wasn't a strong enough word for what I felt for her. It was way more than that. It was an obsession. It was passion. It was most certainly love. And I didn't owe anyone, especially Alcide, an explanation.

Pulling his face back ever so slightly, his sly smile softened. "I'm proud to know that my niece has such a formidable suitor who respects the privacy of their relationship."

My mouth fell open in shock. "Your niece? How is that possible?"

"Her mother was my sister."

Her mother was French, but I had thought she was an only child, not leaving Claire with any family to care for her.

"Camille?" Shyam asked, recalling her birth name from the background check he had run on Claire. There had been no record of her maiden name, almost like it had been erased from history.

"Camille Severin," Mikhail corrected.

Just like Alcide. Through my astonishment, I exclaimed, "Camille was Le Milieu?!"

Alcide nodded. "Much to her disdain. She never wanted the association, but it proved especially useful at times. I loved my sister dearly, but unlike me, she had no desire for the crime world. Our father married her off to a powerful widow who was searching for a new wife. Nicholai knew she was royalty, and after his mess of a first marriage, he wanted someone of higher stature. Someone who understood the role that came with being the wife of a boss. Unfortunately for my sister, her new husband was nothing more than a tyrant who wouldn't dare let his second wife get away with the liberties his first wife had taken."

"Does Claire know about her mother's background?" Shyam asked.

"No. Her mother concealed the truth from her because of Nicholai. He wanted to raise a Bratva child so her loyalty wouldn't be shared when she was an adult and had to make any decisions in her own marriage about which side she would support," Alcide said.

"You helped them escape," I addressed Mikhail. "Did you know of their relation to Le Milieu?"

"Yes. That is the reason I brought them back to France. Camille needed to be closer to her family for the safety of Karina," he said. I supposed, to these two men, she would always be Karina Petrov, even if she never wanted anything to do with that name again.

Alcide continued, "By the time she returned to France, our father had passed away and left the business to me. Otherwise, he would have turned her right around and sent her straight back to Kazan—husbandless and left to fend for herself."

"Has Claire…I mean, *Karina*…ever met you?" I asked.

"I'm afraid not. But I kept watch over her without her ever noticing and with the help of Mikhail," he said, glancing over at the silent man. "It was better that I was a stranger to her so she couldn't ever recognize me as I lurked in the shadows. Camille wrote letters, begging me to keep her daughter safe. She must have known that one of them would eventually wind up dead in Paris. It just happened to be that they got to Camille first."

I remembered that Claire had found her mother's body, slain in their home. The police had ruled it a robbery and that Camille had been in the wrong place at the wrong time. "How did they find Camille?"

Mikhail explained. "They were looking for Karina. I didn't get word about the mission until it was too late and couldn't inform Alcide in time. Karina was supposed to be home at that time, but she returned late that evening because of her dance training."

Seeing her mother lifeless in their home had traumatized her. I had witnessed the fear and paranoia she experienced as a result. If she had only known that Leonid was looking for her that day and that the bullet that killed her mother had really been meant for her, she would never have recovered from the guilt.

"Why haven't you tried to get revenge for your sister if you know Leonid was responsible?" I asked Alcide. If he claimed to have loved Camille so much, why hadn't he tried to punish her killer? He didn't seem like the type who'd be afraid of a young and impulsive Bratva *Pakhan*.

He glared at me, slightly offended that I would assume he had simply let Camille's death go unavenged. "My revenge is coming."

*What does that mean?*

"Does Leonid know that you are her uncle?" Shyam asked.

Alcide nodded. "He does, but I also know things."

I waited for him to explain, but instead, he passed me a stack of letters from the rotting wooden desk.

Leaning into the light from the lamp, I thumbed through the letters as Shyam read over my shoulder. They were from

Camille, addressed to Alcide. I read as she outlined how Leonid overthrew Nicholai and covered up his murder. I read of her fear for her own life. I read of her pleas for her brother to protect her daughter.

My eyes froze on the line that revealed the real kicker of this entire Russian tragedy. How the fuck could this be? An *outsider*…had staged a coup of the Bratva.

"Leonid isn't Nicholai's biological son?" I spoke into the air, not really asking anyone of the men in front of me in particular.

Mikhail answered first. "Yes."

So, this was reason why Alcide and Mikhail were fighting so hard to stop Leonid at every assault he tried to launch.

"Leonid knows this?" Shyam asked.

Mikhail nodded.

I could barely speak because the implications of what this had meant knocked the wind out of me. "Fuck."

"Yes." Alcide pressed his lips together waiting for me to wrap my head around the bomb I had just discovered.

Scared to speak it out into the universe, I whispered my revelation instead: "Claire is the rightful *Pakhan*?" Leonid was a bastard, the product of his mother and a random guard. Claire was Nicholai's only child.

"Now you can see why I needed to protect our queen. I never set you up. I didn't know Claire would be coming to *Semya* that

189

day. My purpose for telling you of Leonid's whereabouts was so you could finish him off once and for all," Mikhail said. He couldn't kill Leonid himself since he would be executed for his crime.

Claire was the last obstacle in Leonid's way. Without her in the picture, there would be no proof against his legitimacy as *Pakhan*. He had been lying about bringing her back to Russia to arrange her marriage. Instead, he wanted her on his home turf to kill her.

The Bratva wouldn't believe us if we went to them with the truth about Nicholai's death and Leonid's paternity. They would think Mikhail was being vengeful against their current *Pakhan* and oust him, or worse. And Alcide, he was a complete outsider to the Bratva, so his words carried no merit. The only proof we had were the words of the mother of their rightful queen.

This was just one more reason I needed to protect her now. Her life was in more danger than any of us had ever realized, and I needed to get back to her now.

# CHAPTER XV

## CLAIRE

A shiver woke me from my slumber—the kind of shiver that pierced deeply inside, all the way to the bone, rattling everything in its wake as it spread through the body.

Sitting up to find my dress completely open and my panties amiss, memories came flooding back. Jai's apology, both verbal and physical, filled my thoughts.

Squinting around my room, I searched for him in the darkness, though the loneliness I felt inside told me what my heart already knew. Switching on the lamp next to my bed only confirmed my beliefs. He was gone.

It had been daylight when he was here, but since then, the sun had set. How long ago had he left? Had he stayed and slept next to me? Or had he waited until I drifted off just so he could slip away unnoticed and without any awkward after-sex conversations?

He had seemed fully intoxicated as he explored my body, but his post-coital actions spoke louder.

I read the alarm clock on my side table, which notified me that I had been asleep for over five hours. *Jesus.* The nights of little sleep coupled with the subsequent earthshattering orgasm must have consumed what little strength I had left.

I wanted to believe that what he did to me meant more than just a quick hookup, but his absence made me question what I had really felt under his touch.

My stomach grumbled from emptiness. It was well past dinnertime, and I would probably have to rummage through the fridge for leftovers that the chef had already packed away for the night. I slipped what remained of my dress off and padded over to my dresser to grab a fresh pair of underwear, yoga pants, and an off-the-shoulder sweatshirt. I decided to lose the bra that I had on since my sweatshirt was thick enough to hide my nipples from Zayn or any of the guards on duty. Plus, these tight bras were driving me crazy. I could feel tiny bumps on my skin from the rash that had spread from the constant chaffing. I needed to buy some bras in my real size. Maybe I could ask Lana to grab me some tomorrow.

After getting dressed and emptying my bladder, I made my way to the bedroom door. As I turned the knob, I met resistance.

Jai must have locked it when he left me sleeping in my underwear, paranoid that someone would walk in on me. I rolled my eyes as I unlocked the door and headed in search of food.

The suite was dimly lit, with only overhead lights over the kitchen island illuminating the space. It was very unlike Zayn or the guards to leave the suite this dark. It was as if no one had been home all evening. It had been hours since Zayn left to run "run errands." Surely, he'd have been back by now.

I couldn't hear the slap of combat boots on the polished floors, though that was a standard evening sound. There was always someone roaming the space, waiting and watching for danger.

A knock on the door nearly sent me jumping out of my skin. I wasn't allowed to answer the door for my safety and never had to. The guards always took care of that. If I ignored it, maybe the person would go away. It was late, so maybe they'd assume the guests inside were asleep.

The knock sounded again, louder this time. I looked around me, willing someone to appear to answer the door. But no one did.

"Zayn?" I called out. Maybe he was in his room and couldn't hear the door.

193

I called out again, shouting this time. But again, no one answered.

The knock on the door became incessant. It was probably the concierge. Maybe it was something important since the visitor wouldn't give up. I mean, if it were someone dangerous, they would have broken the door down by now. Bad men didn't knock.

The floor felt cold on my bare feet as I tip-toed over to the door. I forwent checking the peephole but kept the chain on the door. As I opened it, a toothless smile greeted me through the crack. *Igor*! How the fuck had he gotten all the way up here?!

My pulse skyrocketed. I slammed my entire body against the door to shut it in his face, but he was too strong, pushing back on the opposite side of the door. I rammed my back flat against the wood and used my heels to push, trying desperately to keep out the monster behind it. My strength was no match for his, and my sweaty feet slipped on the marble, failing to give me the traction I needed to exert force.

"Help!" I screamed, hoping to God that someone would hear me.

Turning to my side, I used my shoulder to push harder. Suddenly, the force from the opposite side ceased and the door slammed shut.

Before I could check the peephole, the door came slamming against me, ripped off its hinges, trapping me under it on the

194

floor. The back of my head smashed into the hard stone, causing my vision to blur.

I felt the heavy weight of the wood lift off me, revealing Igor's greedy smirk close to my nose. "Time to go home! Your brother is waiting!"

I knew I was kicking and flailing but I couldn't feel my limbs moving. My head seared with pain.

A sharp pinch on the side of my neck elicited a screech from my throat. I felt my consciousness slip away, until everything was blanketed in darkness.

*** 

My body jolted from side to side, like I was in a small boat being thrashed around the open seas. Every bump and thump jerked my body.

Cold air enveloped me, stinging my nasal mucosa with every inhale. My thoughts were fuzzy, but the searing pain in my airways was enough to revive my awareness. My eyes blinked rapidly, only to register complete darkness each time.

I tried to move my hands to pinch the bridge of my nose to ease the piercing sensation, but neither would budge. They were squished tight to my body. I tried to wiggle them free but instead felt tiny spines prick my skin. My fingers moved languorously, as if they didn't belong to my body. The spines weaved between my digits as I tried to identify their prickliness. The length of the spines bent easily between my fingers, crunching like grass under my touch. I knew this feeling. *Hay.*

Trying harder to yank my hands free now that I knew the substance wouldn't injure me too terribly, I pulled hard. Suddenly, they came free of the pressure that held them down, but I knocked my elbows on something hard. The feeling of pins and needles spread through my elbows and down my arms, rendering them momentarily immobile.

Once the feeling subsided, I rubbed my wrists to increase the circulation in them. I was so cold that my fingertips felt numb. They had felt more sensation wedged alongside my hips, where they had been warmed by my body heat.

Pressing my hands on the hard slab that my head kept hitting with every bump under my body, I tried to identify the covering. My hands slid along the rough surface. The slab extended in front of me. I tried to stretch out my legs, but my bare feet hit the slab too.

*Igor.* His face played like a horror movie in my mind. The scuffle in the suite. The door slamming into me, knocking my head into the floor. The sharp pinch at my neck.

My heart pounded in my chest and dread filled my belly as his words filled my ears like an echo. *"Time to go home."*

"No!" I tried to scream, but it came out as a grunt. My hoarse throat ached.

196

I banged my hands on the slab over my head. "Help!" I groaned out as loud as my voice would allow.

*God, please. Please don't let me be here again.* Tears pricked my eyes as my insides churned. My breaths grew quick, escaping me in pants as the cold dry air scraped my airways.

The bumps eased under me, until they stopped completely. Light peeked through slits in the slab that encased me. Ready to pound on the slab for help again, I quickly changed my mind when I heard voices. *Russian* voices. *Male* Russian voices.

My body suddenly shifted completely left and then completely right, then slammed down, jerking me so hard that my head snapped forward and smashed back on the slab behind me. A loud bang above my head threatened to deafen my ears.

The voices grew louder, almost as if they were shouting at each other. The creaking of wood to my left startled me.

Another loud slam sounded before I went tumbling over onto my belly.

Loud grunts filled my ears as the smell of manure came rushing toward me. Wet noses nudged at my body, bumping into me from all angles. A swarm of pigs voraciously attacked the hay that clung to my body. My hands flew up reflexively to cover my head to avoid them stepping on my face to get to the feed.

A gunshot fired into the air, sending the pigs running away in fits of squeals and screeches. I pushed back onto my heels and scooted backward, knocking into the crate that I had just fallen out of.

Big men marked with demonic tattoos and shaved heads stood in a semicircle around me in the drafty barn, eyes hungry for my blood…or something more. *Bratva.*

The grins on their faces signaled that they were starving for something they thought only I had as they inched nearer. I huddled tightly against the wooden box behind me, knowing full well what my fate was destined to be.

Then the sound of boots crunching neared me. The men heard it too and parted to let its originator through.

*Leonid.*

"*Sestra.*" Sister. He spread his hands wide, welcoming me with open arms. "Welcome home!"

The twinkle in his eye glittered with malice as he bent down on one knee, pushing his face closer to mine. Reading the fear in my eyes, he chuckled in amusement. "You look like hell, Karina."

I tried to push away from his reach, but his fingers pulled on my hair, examining the knots littered with hay. "Finished running, are you? It's nice that you're not trying to disguise yourself anymore. That blonde color was absolutely horrid."

He leaned in close so that I could smell his rank breath. "No strong boyfriend to save you this time, huh?"

I remained silent, praying he'd back off so I could release the breath I was holding inside.

"You have disobeyed the Bratva, and according to our code, you must be punished. Right, boys?" he shouted over his shoulder.

The men behind him cackled with enthusiasm.

"Don't touch me," I gritted out.

"Why are you so stubborn, Karina? Didn't you learn from your dear mother's mistakes? She was just as stupid as you and look at where she ended up."

Rage coursed through my veins at the mention of my mother. She was dead because of him.

Without thinking, I pressed my tongue to the bottom of my mouth, making room for saliva to pool. My tongue lurched forward, launching the sticky spit into his face. I couldn't help grinning with satisfaction as I watched it drip down his cheek before his fingers moved to wipe it away, his green eyes bright with fury.

Then his palm smashed against my face, snapping my head to the side on impact.

"Big mistake, bitch," he roared. "I will teach you to submit to me as your *Pakhan*."

"I will never submit to you!" I hissed.

He stood up, laughing at my brazenness. Turning on his heel and addressing his men, he issued his command before walking away. "Prepare her for her trial."

# CHAPTER XVI

## JAI

**M**y mind was reeling. Claire was Nicholai's only biological child. As Bratva law dictated, in the event of a *Pakhan's* death, the oldest able child of blood was to succeed the old *Pakhan*. Leonid wasn't his. His mother had an affair with Nicholai's guard and was subsequently hung for her crimes. The letters from Claire's mother clearly detailed the intricacies of the affair and the true paternity of Leonid. Apparently, Camille had found the diary of Nicholai's first wife and kept those secrets quiet from everyone except her brother, Alcide.

As if being Bratva weren't shocking enough, Claire was also the daughter of Le Milieu, the most powerful arms-dealing organization in the world. Her blood was royalty. She was the queen of the Bratva.

Men were always the leaders of the Bratva, but there was nothing in their code against a woman ruling. It had just never happened because *Pakhans* always made sure to have many children, increasing their chances of ensuring that a male heir was available in the event of death.

Surely, the men wouldn't take too well to having a woman lead them. The crime world was notoriously chauvinistic. Men ruled with iron fists and women were expected to fall in place. There were female players in our world, but they were few and far between, and none of them were as young as Claire. They were experienced older women who had worked for years to command respect and attention from the men who viewed them as inferior.

Leonid knew that he wasn't Nicholai's biological son. That was why he wanted to get his claws into Claire so badly. He could easily have just let her escape Russia and live out her days in peace and quiet. But that wasn't enough for him. He wanted to ensure that she wouldn't be a complication during his hoax of a rule as *Pakhan*. If she were dead, she would never again be a threat to him.

And Claire didn't know a damn thing. The sweet being just wanted to dance and live a life free of danger. But like her mother, her fate had been sealed the moment she entered the world. She would always be the child of two international crime organizations.

How would she handle the news? It was best that I be the one to break it to her, but I had no idea how she'd react. She needed to meet with Alcide and hear everything from her uncle's mouth, but that could wait. For the moment, I needed to be there for her while she wrapped her head around the truth.

She was safest with me, and I needed to relocate her to my place because I knew Leonid wouldn't rest until he killed her.

After hours of driving back to New York, despite Shyam's speeding and whizzing through red lights, we pulled into the garage of Zayn's building. His car was parked in his assigned spot, signaling he was home, despite my failed attempts to get ahold of him.

I had called him shortly after leaving the warehouse in Boston, but he didn't answer. I sent him multiple texts to let him know to keep a close eye on Claire and that I had news to share. Those messages had gone unacknowledged.

Shyam haphazardly parked to the left of Zayn's car, barely paying mind to painted white lines surrounding the spot because he was in such a hurry to get out. I opened my door but met some resistance. My eye caught a mass on the ground, under my door, keeping it from fully opening. "The car door is stuck. There's something on the ground," I muttered to Shyam.

VICTORIA WOODS

He got out from the driver's seat and went to inspect the issue.

I sat back in my seat, hoping he would move whatever was blocking the door quickly so I could find my woman and start moving her over to my place. Leonid would have to pry her from my dead hands before I ever let her go again.

"Jai, get out here!" I heard Shyam shout through my cracked door. "It's Zayn!"

Jumping over the center console through the driver's door, I came around to where Shyam was crouched over a body.

"Zayn!" I shouted, shaking the massive immobile lump. His chin was bruised, and his clothes were rumpled as if he had been in a fight.

We worked together to push him to a sitting position, leaning his back against his car for extra support. His eyes remained closed as we tried to revive him. I slapped his cheek hard, desperate to bring him back to his senses.

His face turned with the slap, and his eyes squinted from the pain. "Wake up," I shouted. His eyelids relaxed, then lazily opened. Blinking slowly, he finally registered some recognition.

"What happened to you, man?" Shyam asked.

Unable to form coherent words, Zayn groaned in response.

"He's been drugged." I knew it from how drunk he seemed and how dilated his pupils were. "Let's get him upstairs."

Shyam and I flanked him on either side, supporting his weight on our shoulders. His legs wouldn't move with their usual coordination, but they moved just enough for us to drag him along.

We stumbled into the utility elevator, and I fished my spare hotel keycard out of my pocket. After scanning it on the reader inside of the elevator, we ascended to the top floor.

The elevator door opened, and we made our way to the suite.

"What the fuck?" Shyam whispered in shock.

The heavy suite door lay flat on the floor. It had been ripped off its hinges. There was no evidence of guards inside.

"Get him inside," Shyam said.

The smell of metal assaulted my nose and made my eyes water.

We moved quickly toward the couch and deposited him onto the cushions. Shyam raced down the hall to search for any of our men.

My mind was focused on only thing.

"Claire," I shouted, running to her room. The door clicked open, revealing an empty room. She must have woken up and left the room in the time that I had been gone, since it was no longer locked. I bolted to her bathroom and then to her closet, shouting her name.

Shyam's voice caught my attention from across the suite. "Jai! Come here!"

Moving as fast as my feet would allow, I found him inside of the office, frozen to the spot just beyond the doorway.

Dread filled my gut. I was terrified of what I might discover inside. Scared that I might see a vision of Claire that I could never unsee. My shoes tapped on the marble. One step. Another. Then another.

Nine men in all. Our men. Bound and gagged in a heap, their throats sliced and left to bleed out.

The Bratva had been here.

"She's not in here either," Shyam uttered.

They had taken her. *Fuck.*

My lips trembled, too fearful to speak. The tightness in my chest caused me to clutch my heart.

Shyam left the office hastily, grabbing my arm to pull me in tow. We returned to Zayn, to find him more alert than when we had left him.

"Zayn, I need you to tell us what happened. Our men are dead in your office," he started.

The only clue of shock on his face was his eyebrows straining to raise. The drugs were still in his body, dampening his reflexes and leaving him practically emotionless.

He swallowed, his Adam's apple bobbing up and down. "I don't know." His voice came out hoarse and his speech was slightly slurred. "I was on my way back from giving Jai

206

and Claire some space. One of the guards approached me as I was getting out of my car. I thought he was going to report something to me since he looked to be in a hurry, but instead, he bumped into me and then I felt a sharp pinch in my neck before everything went black."

"They must have used a syringe," Shyam said. The attacker must have also sedated the guards before murdering them in Zayn's office, since there was no trail of blood on the marble floors in the rest of the suite. "Do you remember which guard it was?"

Zayn nodded. "One of our regular guys."

"It was an inside job!" I exclaimed. "Leonid is behind this."

"Were you here the whole time?" Zayn asked me, his eyes still looking hazy from his hangover.

I shook my head. "I left Claire asleep hours ago to meet with Mikhail."

"What did he say? Can we trust him?"

"Yes." I filled him in on everything I had learned.

"So, Leonid is a bastard and Claire is the rightful heir to the Bratva?" Zayn's eyes stayed glued to mine. "How can you be sure?"

Shyam took over. "Alcide had letters from Claire's mother."

"Fuck," Zayn gasped.

"Leonid has her. I need to go to Kazan now." I needed to get her back.

207

VICTORIA WOODS

"Are you sure she's there?" Zayn asked cautiously.

I stared at him, my eyes ready to bore holes in him for questioning me. I didn't have time for an interrogation. We had been gone for almost eight hours and were losing even more time sitting here. "I need a burner phone!" I shouted.

"In my nightstand," Zayn offered.

I hurried to retrieve it. I typed in Mikhail's number with the phrase "family reunion at home" for the body of the text as I returned to the couch. He would know that I meant for him to haul ass to Kazan with Alcide. I'd need him there to get Claire back.

Shyam was already on the phone with his security team issuing commands. He hung up just as I finished speaking with the flight team to have them gas up the jet.

"We're taking half the men with us, and the other half will guard Amelia and the kids. They will meet us on the runway with all the ammunition we'll need," Shyam said.

My heart warmed at his support. He had left this world to keep his family safe, and here he was leaving them to come to my aid. "You don't need to come, brother. This is my fight. You should be home with your family."

He reached out a hand to my shoulder, giving it a gentle squeeze. "*You* are my family. They will be safe. Leonid's attention is on Claire right now, so let's get her back and finally end his reign of terror."

208

Too moved to say anything, I offered a faint smile.

"Let's go," he urged.

I was humbled by how much he would sacrifice just to stand by my side. And I never had to ask him to do a thing. *This* was real love.

"I'm going with you," Zayn huffed as he stood up unsteadily from the couch.

"No. You're not in a position to leave right now," Shyam scolded him.

Zayn's usually gentle face grew stern and full of intention. "I'm coming and that's final," he barked.

We didn't have time to argue like this. I supposed he would recover fully on the flight. Maybe the flight attendant could make him a latte or something since he was so obsessed with them.

I nodded.

Wordlessly, the three of us filed out of the suite, prepared for a war. And this one, we weren't willing to lose.

# CHAPTER XVII

## CLAIRE

The Petrov estate. My childhood home, though it felt more like a prison.

The property had been in my family for over four generations and spanned fifteen acres of land. So vast, it offered privacy to conduct Bratva business on the premises.

The palatial monument of a house stood at the top of a hill. The estate overlooked unkempt forests ruled by towering birch trees that crowded together, providing the best scenery for devious men to carry out violent plans.

Though it was only autumn in Kazan, it seemed more like the beginnings of winter with how cold the air felt against my face. Full gray clouds blanketed the early morning sky, and the bitter wind no longer blew forcefully. Snow would be here soon.

The false serenity of the grounds did nothing to quell my anxiety. The abuse I had endured over the past day would be nothing compared to what I was about to face.

The men had taken turns beating me with whips, wood boards, metal rods, and whatever else would inflict pain with minimal effort on their part. This was play for them, not work, and they wanted to enjoy their time using me to remind themselves of the power they held over women.

As if lashing a woman less than half their size weren't enough to make their dicks grow, the men had degraded me too. Their greedy hands had roughly fondled my body in between beatings. One of them, bald and with sharp teeth that reminded me of a reptile's, had tried to force himself between my legs. My stomach had immediately roiled, emptying its contents all over me and spewing onto him as well. After that, no one dared to try again, disgusted by the putrid smell that grew more sour as time ticked by.

Leonid never participated in the bacchanal. As a matter of fact, I hadn't seen him since that first night in the barn. He had allowed his men the honor of tiring me out just to the point of breaking me but not a step further. His revenge would come later when I was too tired to resist.

And I was nearly there. My mind was more exhausted than my body as Igor shoved me through the thicket behind the house. One hand on the ties that bound my hands and another on the rifle strapped to his shoulder, he jerked me forcefully with no regard for the brush that whipped at me as we passed by. My mouth was bone-dry from the gag shoved into it to keep me quiet and the cold air preventing any sort of saliva from being secreted.

The bruises on my stomach ached with each step. The blood from my wounds had crusted over, causing the material of my sweatshirt to stick to the lacerations, which created a ripping sensation every time Igor shoved me. My bare feet seared with pain from the thorny weeds I traversed. In a few weeks, all this flora would die for winter, but lucky for me, it was still alive for now.

We were nearly at the edge of the forest. I could tell by the subtle brightening of light ahead of us, due to the decreasing tree covers. I knew where he was taking me. *The meadow.*

Bad things happened in the meadow. The low-lying grass made it the perfect theater for the men to gather and view whatever show their *Pakhan* had in store for them.

The frost that had accumulated on the grass melted under my feet, causing me to slip as I proceeded further. The cold air bit at my face, making my eyes water.

At the valley of the meadow, lines of Bratva men stood at full attention, dressed in black, awaiting our arrival. All eyes were focused on Leonid standing in front of them. Dressed in a black leather cape with matching gloves, he donned a satisfied smirk on his face.

My eyes flashed behind Leonid, to a large platform that resembled a stage. Two tall wooden posts stood erect parallel to each other, with another post running perpendicular to both at the top in the center of the platform. A lone rope hung from the top beam…with a loop at the end of it. A small crate sat on the stage directly under the rope. This was my final punishment.

My legs froze as we reached the steps to the platform. This couldn't be it. I couldn't come to terms with the idea that this was how my life would end. All the fighting and hiding for years couldn't have been in vain.

Igor grabbed me by my hair and yanked me up the steps, the splinters from the unfinished wood grazing my feet. He stopped in front of the crate on the ground, just in front of the noose above, and turned me to face the sea of men.

"Gentlemen," Leonid shouted loud enough to be heard by all, his voice riddled with excitement, "thank you for gathering here this morning."

The men stared at their *Pakhan* with intense focus.

"We have suffered a great atrocity from one of our own: a child of our beloved Father, Nicholai, and a sister to us all."

Eyes from the crowd glanced to me before returning to their leader.

"Karina broke our hearts when she left us at the very moment when our empire fell to ruins in the wake of the death of our beloved *Pakhan*," he said, his voice somber with false despair. "I worried for years that she was dead somewhere."

The tenor of his voice changed to reflect triumph. "After years of searching, I found her. Unfortunately, she is no longer the sister we once knew. She had become intimate with our enemy, finding her way into his bed."

Murmurs broke out across the meadow.

"That's right. She became a spy for the Sethis. Betraying her blood." His hands formed fists in the air. "As Brothers, we pride ourselves on loyalty and honesty."

I couldn't help but scoff under my gag at the hypocrisy. Igor heard my disdain and knocked me in my back with the end of his rifle, sending me stumbling forward.

Leonid's original plan had been to bring me back to Kazan and use me as a pawn for marriage to grow his empire. But I supposed none of his allies had wanted me since they all suspected I was a spy working for the Sethis.

"Because of her crimes, we can no longer trust our once beloved Karina. I motion for you to cast your votes on her fate."

Raising his voice even louder while enunciating each word, he shouted, "All those who are in favor of the removal of this stain on our legacy, raise your hand in salute."

Simultaneously, the lines of men all raised their hands in the air, sealing my fate.

Slowly, Leonid took the steps up to the platform and approached me. His eyebrows furrowed with mock concern. "They have spoken, beautiful sister." His stumpy fingers brushed my hair away from my forehead before pressing a wet kiss to my skin. "Say hello to your mother for me." A victorious smile spread across his lips before he turned and walked back to his position in front of his men.

Igor swung his weapon over his shoulder to free his hands, then grabbed me by the waist and lifted me onto the crate. As he fastened the noose around my neck, the weight of the rope made my shoulders slump over just to keep my balance.

I bit down hard on the gag in my mouth to keep myself from falling apart. *I will not cry.*

They wanted to see me crumble, to seem weak, but I wouldn't give them the satisfaction. If Jai ever heard about how I died, I wanted him to know that I didn't shed a fucking tear in front of these bastards. If this had happened to me years before I ever met him, I probably would have broken down in sobs by now. He had shown me real love, and I was stronger because of it. I knew there was good in the world and that these men could never truly steal sunshine or silence laughter. Their times would come, whether it was in this life or the next.

216

The crate under my feet shook as Igor clunked his foot onto the edge, preparing to push it out from under me.

The contented look on Leonid's face made me want to spit on him again. And the men, the ones who had molested me and the ones who had stood by and done nothing, made me fantasize impaling them with a molten spear. This was the end of their witch hunt, and if I could, I would have placed a curse on each of them.

Their faces wouldn't be the last thing I saw when I died. I stared up to the sky instead. Small snowflakes drifted lazily from above. *Maman*. At least I would be seeing her soon.

Taking one last inhale to prepare myself, I closed my eyes, imagining running into my mother's arms again.

The crate jerked under my feet, and the scrape of wood on wood startled me—and then I was falling. I fell until the recoil of the noose snapped me back and strangled my windpipe.

No more coherent thoughts. No more complex sentences to speak. Only one word. A name. *Jai*—

A gunshot sounded, and the falling feeling returned, until I smashed into the ground under me.

# CHAPTER XVIII

## JAI

All rational thought exited my brain when I saw that noose around her neck. Igor kicked the box out from under her feet, and my finger pulled the trigger. The rope frayed as the bullet struck it, and her body slammed down to the wood plank beneath her.

The field of men turned, searching for the direction from which the shot had been fired. Igor ran to Leonid's side to protect him, abandoning his post as Claire's handler.

Weapons drew as eyes settled on the smoke still drifting from the gun in my hands. Mikhail moved forward, making his presence obvious, with his hand in the air as a warning for everyone to halt. Whispers washed over the crowd as they kept their guns aimed at me, but no one fired.

"What is the meaning of this?" Leonid barked at Mikhail, his eyes seething with venom toward his Brother.

Mikhail remained calm as he spoke, approaching Leonid and moving away from me and my own brothers and the army of men behind us. He was Bratva and wanted to stand with his men, even though they were being misled by a dictator. "Release her. She is innocent in all of this."

"No! She is a traitor," Leonid screamed.

I watched Claire from my periphery to make sure she was okay since I couldn't run to her side without sending ammunition flying at my sudden movements. Shakily, she moved her hands from behind her back, slipping her feet through her bound arms to bring the binds in front of her body. *Smart girl.* Her hands grasped at the rope around her neck, pulling it forward, desperate to slacken the noose. Her movements were slow and weak, but I was sure she was strong enough to create space in the knot.

Her body heaved as a reflex from the momentary impact on her windpipe. Her diaphragm instinctively sought more air by increasing her respiratory rate. Satisfied with the looseness of the noose but unable to slip it over her head, she pulled on the gag that was wedged in her mouth and slipped it over her head to discard it.

Sitting on her ass, she found me with her eyes, and they widened with shock, followed by relief.

I returned my glare to Leonid, ready to aim fire if he touched her again. "You're the fucking traitor. We know everything," I called out. "Call your men off."

Snickering at my order, Leonid's jaw stiffened with insolence. "What do you know? You've been sleeping with my sister who's been spying on both of us." He inched forward in my direction. "How does it feel being duped by a woman? You had a Bratva woman in your bed and were too stupid to even realize it."

His words didn't affect me. I knew the truth, that she wasn't a spy for him, and nothing he could say would change my mind ever again.

Shyam and Zayn moved in closer to my side, each gripping their weapons. I shouted to Leonid, "You are the one who's stupid. Do your brothers know your secrets?"

The men looked around; confusion etched on their faces.

"Do they know that you've been stockpiling arms and money in Lebanon for the past five years under their noses?"

Leonid's spine stiffened. Whispers radiated through the ranks.

"Do they know that you killed Nicholai so that you could become *Pakhan*?"

Whispers grew louder, to murmurs.

I launched my final blow. "Do they know that you aren't even Nicholai's son?"

221

Shouts rang out from the crowd, and Leonid grabbed his chest as if he had been shot in the heart.

Looking around at his brothers nervously, he tried to assuage them. "You'd believe trash like the Sethis over your own *Pakhan*? Shame on all of you," he spat, a bold effort to spin this to work in his favor.

I addressed his men. "No. You shouldn't believe me. But perhaps you'll believe someone else."

Leonid froze, frightened to see what I had in store for him next.

Our army of men parted behind me, allowing Alcide to pass through. He made his way to the front, just to the side of Shyam, who stood surveying the crowd for any misstep.

Igor glanced at Leonid, as if waiting for him to explain who the visitor was. Leonid's men seemed equally bewildered, since Alcide had rarely ever made appearances outside of France. Everyone knew his name, but very few knew what he looked like.

"Alcide," Leonid ground out through gritted teeth.

"You've been a bad boy, Leonid," Alcide started. He turned to address the Brothers who were hanging on everything playing out before them like it was a car crash. "You have been misled by this man. He is not one of your own. For all these years, you have been following an imposter. His father is one of your own, but not your beloved *Pakhan* Nicholai."

Leonid's eyes bounced erratically around the crowd of Brothers to gauge their reaction, his signature smirk completely erased from his face.

Alcide held up the letters from Claire's mother. "These letters are from my sister, Camille Severin, your former queen, wife of Nicholai."

I glanced at Claire who stood immobile as she listened to Alcide. I wondered what was going on inside of her head. She must have heard about the leader of Le Milieu before because her face was white with shock at the news.

One man from the crowd shouted, "Why should we believe you?"

Leonid latched onto the doubt. "Yes, these are obviously forged," he said quickly, hoping to convince others.

Unfazed, Alcide continued, "In these pages, my sister wrote about Leonid's paternity and his efforts to cover it up. She learned the truth from a diary she found belonging to Leonid's mother. He wanted the throne so badly that he murdered Nicholai just to secure his position. And now he is trying to come after Karina to remove the final obstacle to his tyranny."

Alcide turned to look at Claire, his eyes softening as he saw her in her tattered clothes and the noose around her neck. "My niece, Karina, is the only biological child of Nicholai."

Gasps filled the field at the implication of his revelation.

Alcide turned back to address the crowd. "Yes, Karina Petrov is your rightful *Pakhan*. Leonid was never Bratva royalty to begin with."

"No!" Leonid screamed in horror. His web of lies had unraveled right before his eyes. He drew his gun, aiming it straight between Alcide's eyes, but Mikhail was faster and clocked his own gun, ready to blow the fallen *Pakhan's* brains out.

Zayn slipped out of formation and grabbed Leonid's gun, quickly aiming it at Igor. None of the Brothers moved to defend Leonid or Igor.

Claire stood frozen in place, staring out into the crowd with wide eyes and the noose still around her neck.

Unexpectedly, the men before her all bowed synchronously on one knee to their queen—row after row of Brothers pledging allegiance.

Unsure of what to do next, Claire's eyes searched for me to help her. I moved to the stage to her side, and removed the binds that held her hands together, then I loosened the noose around her neck and discarded it, freeing her of the weight.

Mikhail's voice broke the silence. "What is your order, *Pakhan*? Should this *traitor* meet his death?" he asked, his gun never shifting from Leonid.

She looked at me, hesitating to say the words. I grabbed her hand and squeezed it gently to encourage her to make a decision—one that was solely hers. She needed this closure. To finally have a say in how this would end.

Claire turned to look down at Leonid, holding his terrified glare. I watched as an array of emotions played out in her eyes: anger at him for killing her mother, fear from the new title she had just acquired, and longing for the brother she had never had.

Her voice rang out hoarse but full of resolve. "Yes."

Mikhail's gun fired the shot clear into Leonid's heart, and he crumpled to the ground. No one moved, not even Igor, to hold his hand as life left his body. No one uttered a prayer for the protection of his soul. And no one shed a tear for his demise.

Snow dusted his motionless body in a white film, falling heavier than moment ago.

The stillness of the moment was ended by the collapse of yet another *Pakhan* when Claire collapsed in my arms.

# CHAPTER XIX

## CLAIRE

The mirror on my vanity table hadn't weathered well in my absence. The edges where the wood frame held it in place had blackened and spots had proliferated toward the center, scarring my reflection with dark stains.

The bristles of the boar-haired brush skimmed through the strands of my hair, freeing it of the knots I had collected over the past few days. It was much easier to brush through it now that I'd washed out the dirt and oil in a hot shower.

The scratches on my face no longer bled, but the noose had left a painfully inflamed imprint around my throat. I could see the shades of pink starting to turn a dark red color. A collar of blues and purples would take its place over the next few days.

This morning's light sprinkle of snow had turned into a downpour of flakes outside the window. Everything was blanketed in a sheet of white for as far as I could see. Snow was typical for Kazan in the fall, but this seemed heavier than what I remembered.

My bedroom was just as I remembered it. The same cherry-wood furniture resided inside, in the same arrangement. The room had been kept clean, but some of the wood had aged with time. Judging from the generic look, it had been used as a guestroom after I left, and the maids had tended to it regularly. All my personal effects had been disposed of, probably burned. My ballet posters, fantasy novels, and photos—all gone. Erased, just like Leonid had wanted to do to me.

My brother—no, not anymore—Leonid had finally received the punishment that he deserved, along with his cousin, Igor. I should have felt relieved that they would never haunt me again, but instead, I felt more restless than before. My brain couldn't wrap itself around the idea that just a few hours earlier, I had been at death's door, and now, the men responsible for my terror were the ones who were dead.

It was over. The demons were dead. But I couldn't rest easy. I wasn't like my father, who'd thrived off vengeance and blood.

In fact, the scene had been too much for me to witness. *The blood pouring out of Leonid's chest...* Instead of satisfaction, I had just been reminded of images of Maman dead in our living room.

My knees had given out, and Jai had carried me back to the house before I could have a chance to witness Igor's punishment. I barely remembered the journey back through the forest.

Jai had vacated the entire house of all Bratva men. Only his men were allowed to secure the premises. I remembered his voice issuing commands left and right as he carried me upstairs.

He had tried to settle me down in my father's old room, and as of late, Leonid's, but I protested. I had begged for him to take me to my old room. It was the only place that didn't feel foreign to me in this barren estate.

With the gentlest hands, Jai had set me on my childhood bed and tended to my wounds. His powerful fingers had been feather-soft as he removed my clothes and wiped me down with a wet washcloth, careful not to apply too much pressure to the lacerations on my core. The chaffing from my clothes had made the edges of my cuts swollen and irritated. He had located some antibiotic ointment and gauze from one of the maids and covered my wounds so they could heal. After wrapping me in a clean, white, floor-length silk robe that he found from in the closet, probably an old garment from one of Leonid's whores, he had tied a loose knot around my waist and tucked me into bed.

He had lain next to me as I released the burden of the day into my tears, Alcide's revelations weighing me down. I had begged Jai to stay with me, scared that the solitude would break me.

His arms had wrapped around my body, and I'd buried my head into his chest, inhaling his safe scent. Reassuring whispers about how everything would be alright and how I had been so brave had filled my ears. I had only cried harder, so grateful for this man. I had just been too overwhelmed to settle myself or rationalize everything that had happened.

The realization that the nightmare I had been living since the day I was born was over was difficult to grasp and too monumental to accept easily.

We had stayed that way for hours, stuck to each other, even as I had conceded to exhaustion. I didn't know if he had slept too, but he stayed with me the entire time.

He had ordered some food for me shortly after I woke up, then left me to eat alone so he could meet with Mikhail for a short while.

My stomach hadn't been able to handle the trayful of custards and rich soups that the maids had prepared for me. I had barely been able to stomach a small piece of bread before pushing away from the buffet in front of me.

A little bit of my strength had returned after the much-needed rest, so I'd decided to take a proper shower to busy myself. Then, I had been lucky enough to find this hairbrush and set to taming my mane to keep my mind occupied, though not successfully.

The door clicked open, revealing Jai in the reflection of the mirror.

"You're up," he said gently as he approached me. He looked disheveled. Today's events had taken a toll on him too. The wrinkles around his coffee-colored eyes were more pronounced and his usually tamed stubble had grown longer, completely covering his jaw.

His t-shirt was creased from lying with me, and his jeans were wrinkled.

"How do you feel?" he asked as he tucked his hands into his pants pockets.

I stared at his reflection in the mirror and shrugged. "Like crap. But I can't wallow in it." I had already crawled into a ball and cried my eyes out once for the day. And I was sure I would do it again tonight, so being up and about was probably a good change of scenery for me.

He eyed my mostly untouched tray of food on the bed. "Did you eat?"

"I tried. Not very hungry."

His forehead creased, drawing his eyebrows closer together. "Still thinking about earlier?"

I slammed the brush in my hands down, shaking the vanity table and the trinkets that decorated it. "How could I not?" My voice came out forcefully. "My mother was the daughter of Le Milieu, just like I was the daughter of the Bratva! It was supposed to be me who died first. She died because of me!" The tears heated my eyes once again. "Instead, I'm here as the fucking leader of the Bratva when I don't give two shits about it!" I panted for air as my final words left me.

Jai rushed over to me, stooping down to meet me at eye level. His hands cradled my face. "Your mother did what a parent is supposed to do. She put her child's safety before her own. She might not have wanted this life, but she wanted *you*. She made that clear from the lengths she took to protect you."

His earnestness was what I needed. The way he knew exactly what to say to ease my worry. He was my only refuge in this storm.

He hugged me to his body, and my shoulders instantly relaxed as I exhaled the breath that I had been holding in. His soothing touch leveled my breathing and eased my tears.

I pulled away, still clinging to his arms. "What were you and Mikhail talking about?"

His lips pressed together, and his expression was grim. "What to do about the Bratva."

Dread filled my empty stomach. I was their *Pakhan* now, but it was a job that I didn't want. Leonid had killed for the

232

honor of the title…literally…but here I was, unable to stand any talk of it. I wasn't made for this life.

He hesitated before continuing, choosing his words carefully. "They need a leader. You can't leave them without one."

"I don't want to do it," I answered bluntly.

He nodded, "I know."

"But?" I questioned, sensing he wanted to say more.

"But you have to address your men."

I cackled at the ridiculousness of how it sounded. *My men.* "Those aren't my men. Those *animals* nearly killed me." I felt myself getting worked up again, my voice rising involuntarily to a level higher than that of casual conversation. "They beat me within an inch of my life and tried to force themselves on me. So, no. I don't give a fuck what happens to those cavemen!"

I had already told him what they had done to me, but hearing it again made his jaw clench and his fists tighten just like when he'd heard it for the first time. He had proposed blowing up the entire compound, much to my disagreement. Although I wanted them to burn for what they did, the Bratva abroad would hear word of what we had done and seek revenge for their dear Brothers. We would never be safe again.

"What should I do?" I begged. "Can't you rule them?" Maybe he could just take over the organization like an acquisition or something and rule the Brothers as if they were his own men.

"It's not my place to tell you what to do. You and I are from two different crime families. It wouldn't be right for me to sway your decision. But I will say that I do not want to lead the Bratva either."

Yeah, I guess it was a horrible idea. I was eager for anyone to take the responsibility off my hands, but I couldn't blame him for rejecting my offer. No one in their right mind would be clamoring to rule these savages. Only further proof that Leonid had been psychotic.

"The men are expecting to hear from their queen tonight," he urged.

Fuck. I didn't want to do this. I just wanted to return to New York and never think about the Bratva or Russia again.

"Where is Alcide?" Perhaps my only living relative could offer me some guidance; I didn't have any other family to support me. Sure, he was the most dangerous crime lord in the world, but he was Maman's brother, and she had respected him enough to seek his help when she needed it.

"Downstairs," Jai answered.

"I want to see him." I stared at my robe in the mirror. I would have to change into something a little more presentable before our meeting.

Jai nodded before turning on his heel to bring Alcide to me.

Before he opened the door, I called out, "Tell those monsters that I'll be ready to address them in one hour."

He offered a gentle smile before heading out.

I knew what I wanted to do, but I required input from my uncle first. This was a conversation that I needed to have without Jai present to hold my hand. The new *Pakhan* needed to meet with her peer, the leader of Le Milieu. And these meetings were best held in privacy.

# CHAPTER XX

## JAI

The snowfall had stopped just in time for Claire's address. The sun had already set, leaving the blanket of snow that had accumulated in the meadow to settle for the night. By morning, the white sheet would harden over and turn to ice, covering any evidence of Leonid and Igor's spilled blood.

Torches illuminated the plain, highlighting the ranks of men who had lined up to wait for their new queen.

I stood off to the side, patiently waiting for her to arrive, knowing she would come when she was ready. The weight of her new role wasn't something she could assimilate into within mere hours, so she could take as long as she needed to, as far as I was concerned.

Shyam and Zayn stood alongside me, with our men behind us. Our presence was noticed, so we deemed it necessary to stand on the sidelines out of respect for Claire and her new army.

Mikhail stood tall and proud in the frontline with his Brothers. He was on their side. Always had been. His allegiance had never shifted, despite what everyone thought. He had just been fighting against the injustice that he had witnessed in his brotherhood. The honor of Russia and the welfare of the Bratva were his priorities, and he would have done anything to safeguard them.

Claire had sent word with Alcide after their meeting that she wanted to meet in the meadow to address the men...*her* men.

I hadn't visited her after her meeting with her uncle according to her instructions. Alcide had seemed agreeable after their discussion and bid us farewell before returning to France. Their talk must have been to both of their satisfaction if he were leaving so soon.

The maids had hurried upstairs to help her dress. I wanted to be there to take care of her, but I needed to back off and let her set the pace. Shyam had lectured me on this while we were downstairs. Ironically enough, he was the king of smothering his wife.

The Brothers seemed to be growing impatient in their positions as they waited in the cold. It couldn't have helped that they had outsiders like us attend their private meeting with their new *Pakhan*. But they were forced to hold their tongues since they were guilty of one too many transgressions against Claire. I already wanted to put a bullet in each of their heads for what they had done to her. They might belong to her now, but I would never forget how they had terrorized her when they thought she was beneath them.

She appeared at the head of the valley, dressed in a traditional Russian outfit for queens. The *sarafan*, or gown, that she wore was made of gold silk, so heavy with embroidery that you could see it even in the night. A *kokoshnik* sat on her head. The stiff cylindrical hat was encrusted with rubies and pearls that shined in the light of the torch in her hand. Small strands of pearls dangled over her forehead and gold fabric fell from the bottom rim of the hat.

Her intense beauty was overshadowed by her confident stature. She might have been nervous as hell inside, but it didn't show at all. Her head remained held high, like the queen she truly was.

She walked alone, protected by no one, as if to show that she didn't belong to the Sethi nor the Bratva crime family. She was her own person, not pledging allegiance to anyone.

Taking her place in front of the Brothers, she stood tall where Leonid had stood earlier today.

Flanks of men on both sides were transfixed by the glowing vision of power in front of them.

She spoke in English so everyone in attendance could understand her words. Her voice projected loud and clear into the night, full of authority.

"Men. Your illegitimate *Pakhan* is dead. His greed and ambition launched the bullet into his heart. His disregard for innocent lives secured the final nail in his coffin. But his sins did not die with him. They live on as long as each of you are still alive, as you have each supported him in his tirade.

"In order to appease your *Pakhan*, you waged war against me, an innocent child born unwillingly into your world of violence. Before I fully understood the horrors you inflicted on women and children, you hunted me because your tyrant of a leader commanded it. Not once did any of you question the motives of the one you followed blindly. You murdered my mother, your former queen, in your quest for blood. The leader that you put your trust in misled you and killed your rightful *Pakhan,* Nicholai, and you let him get away with this."

Murmurs broke out amongst the crowd as their heads hung with the weight of her words.

"I suppose you never thought that a lowly woman would one day be your *Pakhan*. But here we are, and each of you have the same stupid, bewildered look on your face."

240

I chuckled quietly at her jest. *That's my girl.*

She continued, "If you take anything away from what has happened here today, let it be that you should be more mindful of who you cross, because tomorrow, they could end up being the person you answer to. Men have fought and died for this throne. And now, this throne belongs to me, a Bratva daughter. But unfortunately, I do not belong to it."

The men looked around in confusion, waiting for her to elaborate.

Her fierce gaze remained forward, as she spoke with finality. "I have called you here to announce the abdication of my throne."

Gasps were audible throughout the meadow.

"I have chosen a new *Pakhan* to take my place. A true leader to you. He has worked to protect your honor and to keep you from bearing the brunt of deceit by your former *Pakhan*."

So, this was what she had discussed with Alcide. Although I had a hunch of who she had in mind, I listened carefully for his name to pierce the blistering cold air.

Claire raised a hand to motion to Mikhail, standing at attention just in front of her.

Mikhail remained still; uncertainty etched on his face while his Brothers looked at him with surprise.

"Mikhail," Claire said as she walked up to him, "will you accept my nomination as *Pakhan*?"

He hesitated before answering. It was the first time I had seen him nervous to speak.

Silence filled the meadow as we waited for his answer.

"Yes, my queen," he declared.

Claire nodded her satisfaction. "All who are in favor of this appointment, raise your hand in salute," she called, her voice echoing throughout the field.

Slowly, as if still unsure of what was happening, each man raised his hand in salute.

A contented grin on her face mixed with a touch of relief that only I could read, she took Mikhail by his elbow and guided him to where she had been standing during her address, in front of his army.

Standing to the side of him, she bowed on one knee to honor the new *Pakhan*, the man who had saved her life all those years ago.

The Brothers followed her lead, all paying homage to their new leader.

Mikhail stood proud like the great ruler he was always meant to be.

I approached the assembly and lifted Claire off her knee by taking her hand, pride bursting in my chest. Her face beamed as she looked at me with a lightness I had never seen in her before now. I loved this strong woman and couldn't believe that she had chosen me to be by her side.

I turned to Mikhail, offering him a silent nod of congratulations. This man had put his life on the line to usher the love of my life to safety when she was a child. He had even risked his neck as my informant, just to protect Claire.

I should have held my tongue, but I needed to know. Leaning in, I asked him so quietly that even Claire couldn't hear, "Claire's mother, she wasn't just your queen, was she? You loved her." He had to have for the lengths he had gone through for her and her daughter.

He didn't answer me but offered a quick twitch of his lips as confirmation. I knew better than anyone that love was boundless.

I turned to the one that I would do anything for. "I love you," I whispered.

"I love you too." She smiled so wide that she looked ready to explode from happiness.

I wanted so badly to kiss her, but not here in front of the Bratva. We had a whole plane ride ahead for me to show her how much I truly loved her. "Let's go home."

# CHAPTER XXI

## JAI

*One month later*

"They're here!" Claire shouted from the living room as I sat behind my office desk, tying up some loose ends. Mikhail had comfortably adjusted into his role as *Pakhan,* and from what little information I had received from my men, the Brothers were satisfied. The Bratva didn't know the extent to which his relationship with me extended, but in my opinion, it had been necessary to achieve a desirable outcome for the organization that Mikhail loved.

If he had never been my informant, Leonid would probably still have been their *Pakhan* and would have driven their legacy into the ground. Now, the Bratva had a leader they could trust and who would put their agenda first. A thriving brotherhood equaled more sales for me.

But all of this meant that I was down an informant, although I supposed that there really wasn't a need for one now, since I had received back pay plus interest for the product that I had supplied them during Leonid's reign. In return, I had resumed regular shipments to Kazan. Business was as it should be—uneventful.

Following Claire's abdication as *Pakhan,* and Mikhail's subsequent coronation, we had all returned to New York. Shyam, Zayn, and I parted ways at the runway. My priority was Claire. She had endured so much at the hands of her own people that I was focused on getting her to my place so she could start the healing process.

That first night home, she had stripped all her clothes off and curled up in the bed under the sheets and slept harder than I had ever seen before. I had let her sleep for a total of twelve hours straight, while I stayed in the house in case she woke up and needed me. When she finally did wake up, I had expected her to need me to hold her or to reassure her again.

Much to my surprise, the first thing she had asked for was coffee. Lots of it. Her demeanor had been surprisingly cheerful, even though her body had been to hell and back. But that was my girl though, tough as nails.

She still had her down moments, too. Some nights, she thrashed around in bed, her body dripping with sweat. The abuse she had suffered in Kazan tormented her. I would hold her in my arms and press my lips to her head to settle her. At first, she had refused to open up about the contents of her nightmares, but after repeated nights of me asking, the dam had burst, and all her deepest and darkest thoughts had come tumbling from her lips.

From then on, I had made a point to create a safe space for her to air her demons. The more she spoke about them, the smaller they would feel to her. The last thing I wanted was for her to spend night after night screaming into the dark, afraid that a man would touch her.

As the weeks had progressed, her nightmares had occurred less frequently. Her latest one had happened five days ago, and I was grateful for her peace of mind.

With lots of care, the bruises and lacerations on her body had healed over nicely, and the mark around her neck was barely visible, too.

We still hadn't had sex yet. I didn't want to burden her with feeling obligated to fulfill my desires while she was struggling. My dick would have to wait; she took precedence now. But it still wasn't easy watching her undress in front of me or towel off after coming out of the shower dripping wet. My mouth salivated every time I saw her bare skin, and my cock raged. Taking care of myself was nowhere near as enjoyable as burying myself into her warm slit. I had the worst case of blue balls and couldn't do anything about it. My hormones would have to wait until she was ready.

"Hey!" Claire poked her head into my office, her hair in a loose bun at the top of her head, locks of honey-colored hair trailing alongside her face. "Everyone's here! Aren't you coming?"

I closed my laptop and pushed back from my chair. "Yup. Just finished here."

She rolled her eyes. "You're such a workaholic!"

"Like you're one to talk," I teased as I approached my girlfriend. She had been busy coming up with plans for a dance school of her own.

Alcide have given her money that her mother had set aside for her, and she had been using it as seed money to jumpstart her business. The school still had a ways to go before opening day, but her passion for the project kept her occupied and gave her a whole new purpose, sometimes keeping her busy well after dinnertime with plans. She was obsessed with her business, and I loved it.

"Your family is going to think you don't want them here if you don't show your face," she scolded me.

Wrapping my arms around her waist and pulling her in closer, I nuzzled her neck. "Good. Then they'll know exactly how I feel." I pressed kisses to the sensitive area under her ear.

Unable to disguise the moan that I'd coerced, her body relaxed into my touch. "We haven't seen them all since before Russia, and I miss hanging out with Amelia."

Amelia had been eager to check in as soon as we returned from Kazan, but I had asked her to give Claire a little space to wrap her head around what had occurred at her childhood home. She'd begrudgingly accepted my wishes but still called me every day to ask a million questions. As annoying as she was being, I knew where she was coming from. She was worried about her friend, and I was grateful to my sister-in-law for caring about Claire as if she were her own family member.

"You like Amelia, huh?"

"What's not to like? She's like the sister I never had. And she has the sweetest children," Claire gushed.

"That, I will agree with. At least until…"

She pulled back, trying to read my thoughts. "Until what?"

*Until we have our own children.* I had never thought I'd reach this place where I was ready to commit to one woman and share my life with her but having Claire in my home…*our* home… felt right. I didn't find her intrusive nor did she make me feel uncomfortable in our shared space. Instead, I enjoyed that I could talk to her whenever I wanted to, and I was never alone.

I wasn't sure when it had started, but I'd often find myself daydreaming about the future—buying her the perfect ring and making her my wife. And children. I wanted nothing more than to grow our family and nurture them in the love that their parents had for each other.

Instead of revealing the dreams that swirled in my head, I shrugged them off. "Nothing."

Eyeing me suspiciously, she broke our embrace to grab my hand and lead me out of the room. "Come on! They're waiting for you!"

The living room was bustling with life. Shyam and Amelia were cozy on the couch, and Zayn sat across from them with a beer in hand. Meena and Dylan were chasing each other around the coffee table, without any regard for people's feet in their way.

"Uncle Jai!" Meena exclaimed, running up to me and squeezing my legs in a tight hug. "Mommy said you went to Russia again. What did you bring me back this time? The twinkle in her wide eyes sparkled brightly as she looked up at me, a skill she had expertly honed to squeeze whatever she wanted out of me.

I grinned at her freckled face. "Your Aunty Claire." I winked.

She studied me for a moment, mulling the new title I had given Claire over in her head. Anticipating some deep question about the relationship between her ballet teacher and her uncle, I braced myself.

To my surprise, her shoulders dropped in disappointment. "So...no chocolate?" she asked instead, seemingly irritated.

"Not this time, sweetheart," I said, patting her head.

She let out an exasperated sigh that was far too big for her body, before returning to her brother to play.

Claire chuckled next to me, just as amused as I was by the tiny tyrant in my living room.

"It's about time," Zayn teased as he stood up to give me a hug. "We were starting to think you didn't want us over."

"Keep raiding my fridge for beers and I'll take back any future invitations," I joked back, nodding toward the bottle in his hand.

"You can never get rid of us. We wouldn't let you," Amelia chimed in.

"And neither would I," Claire agreed. The two of them always backed each other up. They were one member short of being Charlie's Angels or some shit.

I plopped onto the couch and Claire perched herself on the armrest next to me. Dissatisfied with the distance between us, I pulled her into my lap.

"Jai!" she muttered, her cheeks turning red with embarrassment. Her modesty was cute, but our family wasn't the type to shy away from public displays of affection, at least not after Shyam had married Amelia.

"What? Nobody here gives a fuck," I argued.

"Language!" Shyam barked, eyeing his children playing by the fireplace.

I rolled my eyes. "Sorry, Dad."

Conversation flowed naturally over the next hour and thankfully no one mentioned what happened in Russia. Amelia caught us up on her projects at work as Shyam beamed with pride at his wife's ambition. Zayn shared his decision to remain in New York to be closer to us. And Claire gushed over ideas for her studio.

Amelia even offered to help set up Claire's website for the new studio. Even though I was perfectly capable of helping her myself, I was glad when she accepted Amelia's aid so the two could grow their bond together.

"Mommy, I'm hungry," Meena whined, resting her head on her mother's lap for dramatic effect. You would think she hadn't eaten in two days with how pitiful she looked.

"Me too!" Dylan added, looking less pitiful and more like he just wanted to be included.

"Let's go see what Uncle Jai has to eat," Amelia said, using Shyam's lap to push up to stand.

"I'll take them," Claire stopped her. "You relax. I know where all the good snacks are, anyway!" She winked at Meena as she led both kids into the kitchen.

"She looks good," Amelia said as soon as Claire was out of earshot.

I nodded. "She's getting there."

"Does she ever get nightmares?" Amelia knew firsthand about the recovery process after being kidnapped. After we had killed Tarun and she was safe in our home in India, she had still had to deal with the traumatic memories of being a captive. I didn't know the details, but I assumed she had battled nightmares of her own.

I lowered my voice to ensure the conversation stayed in the living room. "They used to be frequent but now they're more sporadic."

She nodded encouragingly. "That's a good sign."

"And how are you?" Zayn asked me before taking another sip of his beer.

"Just trying to get back into the swing of things." My attention was focused on Claire's recovery, but I had a ton of accounts to catch up on since I had been solely preoccupied with the Bratva for so long.

"Mikhail seems to be happy as Pakhan," Shyam offered, running his fingers along the armrest next to him.

"I haven't heard much from him, so that must be a good sign." I glanced over to the kitchen to see Claire reaching for a box of chocolate graham crackers in the shape of tiny bears. She must have bought those because I never kept processed shit like that in the house.

"So, when are you leaving the business?" Shyam asked.

I snapped my head around, shocked by his question, only to meet his expectant stare drilling into me. "Huh?"

"You mean, you haven't thought about giving all of it up?" Zayn joined in.

What the hell were they saying? This was my job. My livelihood. I hadn't once thought about giving it up. "What? No!"

"You and Claire are serious, no?" Shyam continued to grill me.

"Well, yeah." I mean, if it wasn't evident by now, they must have been blind.

"Do you want to marry her?" he demanded.

The room suddenly felt ten degrees hotter and sweat coated the back of my neck. This inquisition was too much to deal with right now, especially with Claire in the next room. "That's my business."

He ignored my brush-off. "She just gave up the Bratva to run away from that life. You think she's going to stick by your side while you make deals with them and meet with criminals every night while she's at home asleep in your bed?"

"Um…" I couldn't come up with a rebuke to his point. "We haven't really talked about all of this yet."

UNCONTROLLED

"You're such a dumbass!" Amelia leaned in, practically yelling at me even though her voice was low. "She's never going to tell you to leave outright. That girl has it bad for you, but she definitely won't be happy if you continue the business."

"What would I even do if I left?" This was the only thing I was good at, aside from programming.

"Come work at Sethi Tech!" she said enthusiastically.

"As what? You took my job, remember?" I nudged her shoulder.

"Board member! You and Shyam built the company; you'll always have a position if you need it."

"Why do I get the impression that you'd be excited to be my boss?" I raised my eyebrow.

"Shyam would still be your boss," she corrected.

"But you basically run shit. So, yeah...you'd be my boss."

"Yeah, but I'm great to work for! Ask my employees," she smirked.

"As tempting as this sounds, I'm not leaving." I was certain that I wouldn't give up my business.

"How bad do you want Claire?" Zayn asked, his tone serious.

I spun my family ring nervously, the one with the Sethi empire emblem, around my finger. "I don't have to answer that." My feelings for her were clear. I wanted her in my life forever, to be by my side as my partner. "And if I left, would you

255

want to take over the business or something?" I asked. Zayn was the only other person capable to run my dynasty. Even though he wasn't a Sethi by blood, the business was just as much his as it was mine.

Zayn shook his head profusely. "Me? No, thanks. I'm not interested in leading. I'd probably take some time off to train overseas again."

Zayn was skilled in combat. As a trained fighter, he had studied all over the world from various masters to perfect his skills.

Shyam interrupted, "You mean you gave me such shit about needing to leave the business for Amelia, and now you won't even do it for Claire? You're such a hypocrite." Shyam interrupted. I had offered him a way out of the business after he had sent Amelia away when the Bratva were after her. He had left the business to me and had settled down with hopes for a quiet life with the woman he loved. But I wasn't him. I was made for this business, and I had no desire to give it up.

Soft giggles distracted me from my brother's judgmental glare. Claire and the kids were approaching us. Before they were close enough to hear me, I whispered with decisiveness to my brothers and sister. "Look, I'm not leaving and that's final." This conversation was over.

# CHAPTER XXII

## CLAIRE

"Today was fun," I said as I fiddled with the back of my earring to free my lobe of the now squeezing pressure. Jai had gifted me diamond studs soon after our return from Russia, and they were the most beautiful pieces of jewelry I had ever seen, yet the most frustrating to remove. These earrings with screw-backs were brutal and always took me forever to take off.

Finally, the small piece of metal came loose in my hand, and I tossed the jewelry into a small dish on top of the dresser.

"Yeah," Jai replied absentmindedly. He was already in bed, completely stripped down and covered from the waist down by the sheets. His chiseled chest was on full display as he sat back against the headboard, his eyes glued to his phone.

"It was great seeing everyone again. We should do that once a week. Maybe host a family dinner or something?" I approached the bed.

"Sure," he responded, not looking up from his device. He seemed irritated, but I couldn't imagine what could have pissed him off. Nothing out of the ordinary had happened while his family had visited. Everyone had left in good spirits.

I pulled the sheets back on my side of the bed and slid under. My black jersey nightie rode up to my waist as I situated myself next to him. I had chosen to ditch underwear to sleep since I hadn't yet gone shopping for properly sized undergarments. I was still using the too-tight ones that Zayn's concierge had purchased for me. I wanted to be comfortable in bed, not having to keep pulling wedgies out of my ass. "Are you okay?"

He put his phone down on the nightstand and focused on me. "Yeah, why?"

"You just seemed a little off toward the end of their visit today. Who pissed you off?" I asked half teasingly.

"No one," he answered abruptly. Before I could continue my questioning, he pulled me on top of him, my thighs straddling his bare dick.

I rested my hands on his chest. "You know you can tell me anything, right?" I could feel him starting to grow against my bare pussy.

"I do." He let out a sigh. "It's just that my family knows how to annoy me. They're very nosy in case you haven't noticed."

His hands roamed from my shoulders, skimming my skin with his fingertips and leaving a trail of goosebumps as he moved down my arms.

"I guess that makes sense." When his hands reached my wrists, I grabbed them in mine and interlocked our fingers. "Family knows best how to push each other's buttons." I didn't know much about family dynamics, but it wasn't a prerequisite to understanding that the people closest to you were the best at triggering you. "But they really do love you."

Breaking contact with my hands, he found my hips and rubbed me against his full-on erection. "I don't want to talk about them right now," he hummed with his signature mischievous grin on his lips.

We hadn't had sex since before Kazan nearly a month ago even though I had resumed my birth control the day after we had returned when my period started. Jai had given me space to heal, and I hadn't tried to initiate anything either. It wasn't because I didn't want to. I was simply scared that the nightmares that woke me up at night would interrupt our lovemaking. They already ruined my sleep, and I didn't want them to ruin our intimacy too.

Cautiously, I let him move me, guiding my hips along his length. The simple action of rubbing against him seemed to activate a muscle memory deeply etched in my brain. Soon, my hips found their own rhythm, rocking back and forth of their own volition.

"I want you." His eyes burned brightly with need.

I wanted to give into him, but I was scared that visions of what happened to me at the hands of the Bratva would rip me away from the pleasure I felt with him, subsequently ruining the chemistry between us. They had tried to break me, and I didn't want that to break *us*.

My voice shook. "I'm scared."

"It's just me, baby girl," he reassured me. "No one else. And you can tell me to stop at any time," he said gently.

I nodded, willing to try because of my trust in him.

Pulling my head down to meet his, he locked me into a scorching kiss. I lost myself in the feel of his lips moving against mine, his tongue dipping into my mouth.

The pulse of his dick under me signaled it was ready to bury itself inside of me, but Jai didn't move to push me onto the bed. He wanted me to set the pace, careful to never take from me what I wasn't ready to give.

But here in the privacy of our bed, bound together, the demons couldn't touch us. My thoughts and emotions were more present than ever, never once allowing nightmares to slip into my mind.

We ground against each other in perfect harmony, his rigidness providing the much-needed friction my clit begged for.

His hands slid up under my nightie, finding my breasts under the fabric. Calloused fingers worked my mounds, massaging them with a pressure that felt like heaven. His fingertips rested on my nipples as I moved on top of him, causing a gentle rubbing sensation across my areolas. The feeling left me panting with lust.

I pulled the dress over my head and threw it onto the floor, fully exposing my body to him.

"God, you're so beautiful," he exhaled as he raised up enough to kiss right over my rib as his hands continued to knead my tits.

I slid along his length as I stroked against him, my arousal coating our skin. My pussy was ready, judging from how wet she felt.

Pushing up onto my knees, I felt between us for his cock. His serious eyes watched me, waiting to see what I would do.

Pumping his shaft in my hands, I watched as he struggled to keep his focus on me when I knew he wanted to close his eyes and savor the feeling. I kept tempting him with each pump, waiting for him to cave to my control. He tried to hold out but succumbed to me when I increased the pressure of my grasp around him.

Grinning with satisfaction, I gazed at him as he tipped his head back, fully submitting to my touch.

Positioning him at my entrance, I slid down his length in one quick movement, my juices lubricating my walls. His eyes snapped open as he groaned with pleasure. I shuddered at his fullness.

I moved, slowly at first, to acclimate to his size. Every girl probably thought that the man they loved had the biggest dick ever, and I was no exception. I was confident that Jai was bigger than most men, and I was the one lucky enough to reap the benefits.

As my muscles relaxed around him, I moved faster, riding him. The sensations built inside of me, already nearing explosion. I held my breath, scared that my orgasm would slip away just as quickly as it was building.

But it never dissipated. Instead, it detonated, sending my nerves exploding with euphoria as I came around him. "Mon cher!" I cried as I collapsed onto his chest.

Not wasting a moment, he flipped me over onto my back, still impaling me with his throbbing cock. Unapologetically, he pounded into me. It was as if he had just been waiting for me to go first, ensuring that I felt completely safe before unleashing on me.

He slammed harder into me each time, his skin slapping against me almost painfully—treading the line between pain and pleasure.

Sweat dotted his forehead as he held me down and drove into me. His cock thickened, pressing even harder against my walls. Then sweet release overtook him as he grunted and groaned his elation, filling me with his warmth.

He withdrew from me and lay back onto his pillow, catching his breath. I nestled against him, my head resting in the crook of his arm and my fingers gently stroking his chest. We were a sticky, sweaty mess, but I didn't care. The intimacy between us was finally complete and whole again, better than it had ever been before obstacles were thrown at us.

"Did that feel okay?" he asked as soon as his breathing returned to baseline.

"More than okay," I purred. "You can do *that* again whenever you want to."

"I might need a rest and some electrolytes before round two," he teased. "You nearly killed me there."

I chuckled. "I love you," I murmured lazily into his chest, the first hints of exhaustion taking hold of my body.

"I love you too, baby girl," he replied, pressing a kiss to the top of my head. "You should sleep. You sound tired."

As if on cue, I let out a big yawn. "I am. I need to meet with the architect tomorrow to go over the plans for the studio."

"Excited for it to open?"

"So excited." We were still a few months away from opening day, but I couldn't wait to start teaching in my very own school. The seed money that Alcide had given me had been a blessing; and I couldn't have done it without the savings my mother had put aside for me.

"Teaching really is your passion," he said.

"Yes, I love that I get to teach the younger generation something new and hopefully make an impact on their lives."

"That's beautiful." He pressed another soft kiss to my head. "Your students will never forget you as they continue their journey in dance."

The thought of being a part of them even as they surpassed my skill level made me smile. "What about you? What does the future hold for Jai Sethi?"

We hadn't discussed his plans now that the Bratva were no longer a problem. He had resumed work in his business, making new deals with crime organizations, taking phone calls from other drug lords. It was as if the events of the past few months hadn't rattled his impression of the underworld, like he still didn't grasp how dangerous his job was.

He shrugged under me. "My business, I guess. Maybe expanding it to include different products."

"World domination?" I joked half-heartedly.

"I suppose." His answer was bland.

"Do you think you'll always do that *job*?" I posed.

He hesitated for a moment before answering. "I never really saw myself doing anything else."

"Oh." I grew quiet, mulling over the realization that he would never give it up, not even for me. How did I fit into his life plan? I surely couldn't be part of a life that included the underworld again. But was I ready to end our relationship over it?

"What's wrong?" he asked sensing my turmoil.

"Nothing," I replied, pretending that a storm of emotions wasn't raging inside of me.

"You know you can tell me anything, right?" he pressed, using the same words that I had uttered earlier.

"I do." Instead of bearing my soul, I side-stepped the topic. "I think I'm just tired."

The gentle strokes on my arm stopped. I sensed he wanted to say something more, to convince me to open up to him.

But he didn't.

Thank God because I wasn't ready to verbalize the ultimatum in my head just yet. I wanted another night wrapped in his arms before I ripped off the bandage and shared how I really felt.

# CHAPTER XXIII

## CLAIRE

I t had been a week since our talk about Jai continuing his cartel business, and we hadn't spoken about it since. Although we both remained silent on the subject, the tension was thick between us. Or maybe I had just been so caught up in my own thoughts that I had imagined that the friction was two-sided.

I knew I had to get over my fear of conflict and confront the issue. We were already in this too deep. Our first breakup had been torturous for both of us and even that hadn't stuck for too long. We couldn't keep away from each other. I didn't want our relationship to end in another breakup where we continued to fuck occasionally. I hated when people continued in relationships like that. You could never truly move on and leave behind what you deemed as toxic if you kept fucking. A clean break between us was necessary if he wasn't willing to give up the business.

Ultimatums never ended well, but I didn't really see how I could stay if he still had relations with the underworld. I had given up my role as *Pakhan* because I didn't want any part of it. I certainly wouldn't want to be the girlfriend, or even wife, of the leader of the world's biggest drug empire.

The part that held me back from bringing it up was that I would be asking him to choose between me and the family business that his father had passed down. Who was I to make him choose? I didn't even have a ring on my finger or his child in my belly to validate making such a request.

Instead of facing the issue, I poured myself into the studio, harping over every detail.

My current obsession was the plans I was reviewing to give final approval to the architect to proceed. He needed my approval by Wednesday, and it was already Monday, which wasn't much time for me to evaluate everything.

I didn't have an office of my own, so I used the dining room table as a makeshift desk. Blueprints littered the table and the spare laptop that Jai had given me was open with the mockup of my new website.

The sun hadn't risen yet when I rolled out of bed and silently padded into the kitchen, leaving a sleeping Jai behind. He wasn't an early riser since most of his business was conducted late into the night.

I tied my hair up into a messy bun, put on a pot of coffee, and set to work early since I had to meet with Amelia later in the day for lunch, which would shave an hour off my work time.

I worked for two hours before I heard the shower running. *Strange*. Why would Jai be showering at 7 a.m.? He usually worked out soon after waking up, but never showered before heading into his home gym. Ignoring the distraction, I focused on my work.

"Morning, baby girl," Jai greeted me a little while later, dressed in a black blazer, fitted white t-shirt, and designer jeans that hugged the curves of his ass in all the right ways.

"Where are you off to so early in the morning?" I asked, raising my eyebrow.

He busied himself in the kitchen, pouring coffee into a thermos and sealing it with a lid. "Work," he answered matter-of-factly as if he did this every day.

"So early? I thought you didn't work before noon." I was completely stumped, and he wasn't giving me much of an explanation.

He turned around, leaning against the island in the kitchen, still within plain view of me, and flashed me his most charming smile. "I have a new job I'm working on."

My stomach twisted with dread. If he was taking on new jobs, then there was no way he would even consider leaving his business. My heart pounded in my chest, and I blinked quickly to fight away the tears that threatened to fall.

He must not have noticed any of the emotions that ripped through me because he approached me casually. "I better get going before I'm late." He planted a gentle kiss on my forehead. "Bye, baby girl."

He turned and walked out the door, leaving me too stunned to say anything.

***

"Hey, lady," I said as I ducked my head into Amelia's door.

"Oh, hi!" she greeted me from behind her desk, removing the black frames that sat on the bridge of her nose. "Come in!"

I walked over to the chair across from her desk and sat down.

I had never been to her office before, so when she texted me yesterday to invite me to lunch, I had jumped at the chance. Amelia had turned out to be such an amazing friend to me, almost like a sister. I enjoyed her company, and she made me feel at ease.

Her office reflected her style. Lots of black and white accented with metallic colors. She looked like the girl next door, but her style was masculine. I figured her tech background had done something to influence her taste.

"Thanks for inviting me to lunch," I said, taking in the vibe of her office.

"Jai said you've been cooped up in that house all day going over your plans for the studio, so I figured you could use a break."

"Yes, definitely." I also needed a break from the myriad of depressing thoughts that raced through my head lately, concerning my future with her brother-in-law.

"Everything going smoothly with the construction?" she asked.

"Oh yeah. I'm working on a tight schedule to get the plans approved by Wednesday for the architect. So, I've been a little stressed out, I guess."

"I bet. Did you like the mockup of the website?" She had offered to set up a very modern and easy-to-use site that parents could use to register their children and keep up to date with studio announcements. It was exactly what I needed for the school.

"Yes!" I nodded appreciatively. "I love it. Thank you so much for doing that. I'm sure you've been crazy busy here, so I really appreciate it."

"It's no problem at all. Let me know if you find anything you want to adjust. You can just email me your changes." Her gentle smile ensured me that she didn't see it as an inconvenience.

"Will do!" I agreed.

"How's everything else? Are *you* okay?" She was probably referring to the nightmares. They were rarer now, playing their ugly images occasionally.

Amelia had been kind enough to be a sounding board for me since she had been through a similar situation. Her experiences had helped me to recover from the terrible dreams faster since I knew I wasn't alone.

"Just taking it one day at a time. I haven't had a nightmare in about a week," I grinned.

"That's wonderful!" She clapped. "And how's my brother-in-law treating you?"

I froze for a moment, stopping myself from spilling my guts about my worries about his business. "Everything's great," I said, plastering a fake smile on my face.

"Uh-oh. What's wrong?" Her concern turned into the feistiness I had often seen in her own daughter. "Tell me how hard I need to kick his ass."

I didn't want to share too much because he was her family, but at the same time, Amelia and I were so close that I couldn't lie. "It's his job."

"The drug business?" she whispered, eyeing the open office door for any listening ears.

"I don't know if I can stay by his side while he continues doing..." I glanced at the open door before continuing, "what he does."

She nodded in understanding.

"I completely understand that it was passed down in his family and he feels some sort of obligation to continue the legacy, but I don't feel comfortable being involved in it, even if it would be indirectly. What if a disgruntled client decided that he wasn't happy with Jai and decided to..." I couldn't finish the sentence. The thought was too much to bear.

Her forehead wrinkled with concern. "Have you spoken to him about it?"

I shook my head.

She leaned in closer over her desk. "You should. I'm sure he'd understand."

I shrugged. "I can't make him choose. That's not fair to him."

"I think if you just shared what you told me, he'd understand where you're coming from."

I wasn't as confident as she seemed to have been. "But he seems to be in too deep with the business still. He woke up early to meet with some new client today. If he's taking on new clients, then how would he possibly consider leaving?" The man I saw this morning was one who was determined to finalize

273

whatever deal he had been working so hard to secure instead of retiring early. A beachfront condo in Boca Raton and Sunday brunches over the water were the furthest things from his mind.

Amelia checked her phone for the time and stood up from her desk, aborting the heavy conversation all together. "We should get to lunch soon. I ordered us a special meal and the staff are probably waiting on us to serve it."

"Oh, yeah. Sure." I followed her out of the office and down the long hallway in front of us. Her door was the first on the right, but instead of leaving the way I had come in, we kept walking.

"Is this the way to the dining hall?" I took in the sleekness of the glass doors and windows of the conference room we passed.

"I need to stop somewhere first. Is that okay?" she asked.

"Of course." I was honestly so excited to be walking around with her in her element. To think that she ran most of this company amazed me and I admired her ambition.

We passed another glass door on our right.

"This is Shyam's office," she announced. I also read his name on door plate for further confirmation. His door was closed, signaling that he was probably in a meeting.

We continued until we reached the last door at the end of the hall. The name plate was blank, and the door was closed. Amelia knocked.

"Come in," a familiar deep voice called out.

Amelia opened the door and motioned for me to enter first. I had thought I'd just wait in the hallway, not visit her coworker's office.

Not wanting to seem rude, I entered, but I did a double take at what I saw inside.

I froze mid-stride when my brain registered what it had witnessed. "Jai." His name stumbled shakily off my tongue.

Behind the grand black desk sat my boyfriend in the same clothes he had left the house in this morning, his thermos resting in front of him.

I turned around to look for Amelia. Her head poked through the doorway, a cheesy smile on her face. "Bye!" She waved before shutting the door and leaving us alone.

I was finally able to pick my jaw off the floor to speak. "What are you doing here?"

"Working." he grinned.

"But…what…huh?" Words failed me. "I thought you were meeting a new client."

"I was. Just finished my phone meeting with him." He tipped his scruffy chin toward the phone on his desk.

"I don't understand." I kept my voice low so no one passing by could hear, I asked. "Are you using Sethi Tech to meet with other drug dealers?" I couldn't believe Shyam would allow his brother to expose his wife to danger like this.

275

He stood up and walked over to me. "Baby girl, I work here now," he clarified.

I searched his eyes for answers. "But I thought that business was your legacy. You said that it was what you pictured yourself doing in the future."

"Why are you finding this so hard to believe? I gave it up because you're my future now." His hands gently squeezed my biceps. "You're my life and your happiness means more to me than a job."

I couldn't shake my disbelief. I had been struggling with how to broach this topic for days, stressing myself out because I had been so sure that our future would end in our demise because of my ultimatum. "How did you know that I was struggling to talk to you about this?" I whispered.

He leaned in and pressed a kiss to my forehead, his spicy scent enveloping me. "I just knew."

"Did you do this for me? Because I understand that this was your father's dream for you, and I felt like shit asking you to leave it behind for me." Here he was, giving me everything I wanted, and I was just babbling on and on, feeding him reasons to change his decision.

"Does it matter why I did it?" His chocolate eyes pierced mine. "All that should matter is that I want to build a life with you."

I wrapped my arms around his neck and planted a huge kiss on his lips, so thrilled by it all. "Is it really true? You really are done with it?" I had to make sure one last time that my ears hadn't deceived me.

"It's really true. Your uncle decided to take over the business for me," he said.

I leaned back in surprise; my arms still wrapped around his neck. "Alcide?"

He nodded. "He was more than elated to add my thriving drug empire to his existing arms business."

I pulled him in for another kiss, this time longer and full of tongue. My body was bursting with joy.

"Plus, now I have a legit office where I can bend you over my desk in the middle of the workday," he murmured against my lips.

"Careful, I know your boss," I teased. "And she won't appreciate you fucking on the job."

He chuckled. "Technically, Shyam is my boss, but just don't let Amelia know that."

So overcome with happiness by his decision, I pulled myself into his chest, burying my face. I inhaled his aroma and exhaled all the anxiety over our future that I had been carrying with me like a sandbag that had weighed me down for far too long.

His hand rubbed my back gently. "I made you that happy, huh?"

I nodded into his shirt.

"I should leave my drug business everyday if it makes you smile like this!" he teased.

I giggled. His sacrifice without me ever having to ask him to do it meant the world to me. I guess that was what people did for each other in loving and committed relationships. The happiness of your partner became the most important thing in the world.

"I'd do anything for you, baby girl," he whispered as he held me in his arms.

*And I would do anything for him.*

I backed away from his body and walked over to the desk, flashing him a cheeky grin. He watched me with confusion written over his face.

I lifted the hem of my denim mini skirt up to my waist, revealing my black thong. My palms rested on the glossy surface of the desk as I bent over, my ass on full display for him. With only my head turned in his direction, I watched as realization dawned on his face, followed by that cheeky smirk I loved so much.

In my huskiest voice, I issued my order: "Lock the door and black out your windows."

I really would do anything for him.

# Epilogue

*One year later*

"**P**lié. Un. Deux. Trois. And, *tendu!*"

Ten pairs of small legs covered in pink tights mimicked my motions as I supervised their form in the reflection of the mirror in front of me.

"*Très bien*, girls!" I smiled with approval, as the parents in the back of the studio filed in one by one to wait for the girls to be dismissed. Some of them had their cameras out, recording their little ballerinas so they could replay the videos later for anyone who would watch as they fawned over every move.

The pride on their faces was the same look that I had seen on Jai's when my doctor confirmed what my husband had already known on the ultrasound monitor: that we were having a baby boy.

My hand rested on my belly as my little boy kicked with glee to the beat of the music blaring on the studio speakers. He always came to life when music played loud enough for him to hear inside of his little cocoon.

We hadn't been actively trying to get pregnant. Jai and I both wanted children, but I'd wanted to enjoy our time together as newlyweds. So much had happened in our relationship that I had just wanted a moment for us to finally relax into our new roles of husband and wife.

Though, being married to Jai was anything but relaxing. The man had the sexual appetite of a dog with its balls still intact. He had already been too much to handle before we were married, and he had only become even more ravenous since marking me with a wedding band around my ring finger.

Assuming my new role as Mrs. Sethi involved me assuming every position outlined in the Kama *Sutra,* and even creating new ones. I was a flexible woman, but even my body was put to the test whenever Jai started with me. Between the full-time job of spreading my legs and preparations to open the studio, my scattered brain had forgotten a tiny white pill…or two… okay, five!

But in my defense, I had been so busy at the time, I had barely remembered to eat lunch and hydrate most days. So, when I started getting symptoms, I had just thought I was tired and nauseous from burning the candle at both ends, until my period was about two weeks late.

After an urgent text to Lana that I was late, she had immediately come over with a two-pack of pregnancy tests and a bottle of wine on the off-chance both tests were negative. My urine had barely soaked the stick before two pink lines streaked across the little window. Seeing them, Lana had promptly chugged the wine straight out of the bottle, leaving me shocked and sober as hell.

That evening, I had paced the bedroom for what must have been hours before Jai reached home. Worry had wrinkled his forehead when I could barely find the words to explain my state. I had been scared that he would be upset that I hadn't been compliant with my birth control or disappointed that our time as newlyweds was over. Instead, he had lifted me off the ground and spun me around in excitement.

I couldn't have been more wrong about his feelings. He had immediately addressed the baby as "him" because he knew it would be a boy and wouldn't hear any arguments against his beliefs. Months later, at our twenty-week ultrasound, my doctor had confirmed Jai's belief, that we were having a boy, and Jai had beamed with pride as he stared at our son bouncing on the screen.

The glowing look on my husband's face never disappeared. I still saw it every morning when he woke up next to me and placed his palm over my giant belly to feel his little man kick in response. In another month, that pride would be even stronger than before when he held our baby in his arms.

As blessed as I was to be carrying our little miracle in my belly, dancing proved to be harder in my third trimester.

My first trimester had gone smoothly, and I had been able to continue my teaching schedule without making any adjustments. I had, however, rushed home after my last class each day and changed out of my dance clothes to collapse onto the bed and sleep for twelve hours straight. It had been exhausting.

Things were better during my second trimester. I had felt invincible again, able to dance with my students with no loss of energy.

But this last trimester, it was something else. My belly had taken forever to show, but when it finally had, there was no going back. My body didn't feel like my own and my movements were clumsy. I couldn't walk without waddling. I had decided to cut back on my schedule and only teach the younger kids, which required less strenuous movements.

As uncomfortable as I felt, I was thrilled the studio was thriving. Many of my students from my previous studio had switched over to my school. At first, I had instructed all the classes personally. But since the waitlist for entrance had grown so long, with students waiting for spots to open up, I had decided to hire two more teachers. This turned out to be a good move, since I was now relying on those teachers to conduct most of the classes. I would probably need to hire another teacher to cover my maternity leave, too.

"Aunty Claire, when is class going to be over?" Meena's voice interrupted my instruction. "I'm so thirsty!" She stood staring up at me in her pink leotard and matching tights, her arms crossed over her chest.

I had thought she had attitude before, but ever since she turned seven, she had become even more feisty. There would be no hope for Amelia by the time eight rolled around.

I couldn't stoop to her level anymore because of my belly, so I just looked down at her. "Meena, in class, you are to call me Madame Sethi. We must remain professional in the studio," I said softly. "Outside of class, you can call me Aunty Claire."

She stared at me as if I had just grown two heads. "Fine," she sighed, rolling her eyes.

Meena's outburst had burned through my final minutes of class anyway, so I decided to just end there.

"Okay, class. Be sure to practice your splits for next time!"

I reunited each girl with her parent and waited for everyone to file out.

"Can we go now…*Aunty Claire*!?" Meena tapped her foot as if I were wasting her time. She really was a piece of work.

"Yes, we can go."

I grabbed our bags while Meena turned off all the lights. We walked out the door, and I locked up. I held my niece's delicate hand in my bloated one as we made our way to the car waiting for us.

My fingers had swollen up so big that I couldn't wear my wedding ring anymore. I missed twirling it on my finger. Jai had wanted to buy me a fancy ring with tons of diamonds around it, but I'd begged him to keep it simple. A band was enough, especially since the engagement ring he had surprised me with was over the top with a five-carat solitaire diamond.

The engagement ring, however, was definitely not an indicator of the extravagance of our wedding. Jai and I had agreed that it should be an intimate affair with only his family in attendance. I didn't have much in the way of family of my own.

The only living relative that I had was Uncle Alcide, and there was no way he would have left France for my wedding. He would always hold a special place in my heart because of

284

his relationship to my mother and how he had protected me all those years, but he was still tied to the underworld. In fact, he was more powerful than before since he had acquired Jai's drug business. An event with children in attendance was not an appropriate place for a powerful kingpin to socialize. Uncle Alcide had sent his best wishes in the form of a gift: a pair of champagne flutes made of the finest crystal and encrusted with diamonds around the base. I would always be too nervous to use such a lavish gift, but I appreciated the gesture.

The wedding had taken place on Jai's beautiful upstate estate during winter. Jai's entire family had driven up with us for the weekend. My maid of honor, Lana, had even made the trip too.

We had spent all morning getting ready in one of the guestrooms, drinking champagne and listening to music while hair-and-makeup staff had worked their magic on us. Angela, Amelia's mom, had kept the kids busy with activities, giving Amelia an opportunity to get ready for the wedding in peace. The men had been on the opposite side of the manor, probably drinking scotch and smoking cigars up until the last moment before showtime.

Amelia and Lana had helped me with my dress: a floor-length, slim-fitting gown with heavy beading that flared ever so slightly below my knees. I had worn a white faux-fur stole around my shoulders to keep warm, as well as snow boots on my feet since they would be covered by my dress. In keeping with the glamourous theme of my gown, I had requested a red lip with a cat-eye from the makeup artist...

\*\*\*

When my makeover was complete, I stood in front of the mirror. It wasn't the sophisticated makeup and elegant gown that caught my attention—it was the expression on my face. My smile reached my eyes. No longer did wrinkles crease the corners of my eyes from stress and anxiety; now, they adorned my eyes from happiness. I saw my mother staring back at me in the mirror, but with far less worry written on my face than she had always had. My only regret was that she wasn't here to walk me down the aisle, but I knew that she was watching over me from wherever she was right now.

It was finally time.

Snow blanketed the grounds around the manor, and the skies were clear of storm clouds, allowing blue skies to embrace the yard. A very brilliantly dressed Angela met us at the French doors at the back of the house with her grandchildren bouncing around in excitement.

Dylan, our ring bearer, looked so adorable in his little tuxedo and perfectly styled hair. He was the first to walk down the aisle, with his grandmother at his side. He clutched a small wooden box that contained the wedding bands as he trotted through the partially shoveled path to the wooden gazebo where the men waited.

Meena was next. Our flower girl glowed in her dress, burgundy velvet material above the waist and matching tulle from the waist down. She left a trail of red rose petals behind her as she took her seat next to her grandmother.

My maid of honor and my bridesmaid looked beautiful in their burgundy dresses and bouquets of winter greens and holly. Amelia walked down the aisle first, followed by Lana, through the trail of white snow.

I clutched the bouquet of white roses, winter greens, and red holly in my hands as I waited for my entrance music to begin. The first strings of the violin sounded, signaling my turn. I closed my eyes and took a deep breath, letting the cold air purify my lungs. Opening my eyes, I focused on my feet, ensuring that I exited without tumbling over the doorway. My feet stopped as soon as they crunched into the inch of snow that had been left behind by the event planners to make walking easier while "keeping the winter vibe."

I looked up before heading down the path, and that's when I saw him. The love of my life. My breath caught as I took in the vision of Jai in his black tuxedo, the picture of refinement. Although he wasn't a part of the criminal world anymore, the dark stubble on his jaw and neck gave him that look of danger that attracted me to him. His chocolate eyes were focused only on me and alive with enough fire to warm me even in the cold air.

I kept moving, needing to be closer, never breaking our connected gaze. I wasn't sure how long it had taken me to reach him, but I knew that I was finally home when he took my hand in his and Zayn began the ceremony as our officiant. He kept the ceremony short and even peppered it with a few jokes that elicited laughs from everyone, including Shyam, who stood behind Jai as his best man.

I hung on Jai's every word as he said his vows to me before placing a simple platinum band around my ring finger. I returned the gesture as I promised to be his forever. Zayn pronounced us husband and wife, and we sealed our commitment to each other with our first kiss as a married couple. Jai wrapped me in his arms as our lips found each other and parted ever so slightly to allow our tongues to meet, but just a little to keep from being obscene in front of the children. The entire party clapped and cheered in approval as my husband and I walked back to the house and the photographer captured the beginning of our life together.

*\*\**

That day had been so perfect that I had told Jai I wanted to spend every anniversary at his manor to celebrate our marriage.

The car came to a stop at the curb, tearing me away from my blissful memories. Our home was only eight minutes away from the studio, but Jai insisted that we use his driver. I would have thought his overprotectiveness would have faded by now, but instead, it was stronger than ever now that I was pregnant. I was scared to think how bad it would get once the baby was finally here.

I got out first, before helping Meena out. I fished my keys out of my bag to let us into the house.

Loud voices greeted as us as we walked through the penthouse I shared with Jai. Everyone was already here.

"Uncle Jai," Meena exclaimed as she ran into his arms.

My husband wrapped our niece in his strong arms and pressed a peck to her head. "Hi, princess!"

Meena ran off to greet Zayn, who sat around the dining table with her mother, father, and brother.

"There's my wife," Jai greeted me, pressing a kiss to my lips. That look of pride brightened his face again as he bent over to kiss my belly. "And there's my son. Have you been behaving for Mommy?" he asked gently, rubbing his hand over my bump.

"He's been an angel, kicking my bladder all day," I joked sarcastically.

"That just means he's getting those legs in shape to be a football player." He chuckled, taking the bags from my hand, and setting them down.

"Hey, everyone!" I said to the gang. "Did you guys start dinner without us?" I said eyeing the spread on the table. My stomach growled on cue. This baby was always hungry.

Zayn stood up from his seat and pulled it out a little more so that I could sit down. I took it gratefully. He pressed a kiss to my cheek to greet me before finding a new seat.

"No, we were waiting on you guys," Amelia said as she started dishing out food onto plates for the kids.

"How are you feeling?" Zayn asked. Dylan bounced in his seat next to him trying to coerce his uncle into a round of horseplay before dinner.

"Not too bad." I grinned. "I just feel big. And hungry."

"Then, let's eat!" Amelia hurried everyone to take their seats, and before I knew it, we were all shoving forkfuls of delicious roasted chicken and mashed potatoes into our mouths.

"Oh, by the way," Amelia started. "I brought you more stuff for the baby. It's in the nursery."

"You shouldn't have," I pouted. "You've done so much already,"

Amelia had been so helpful from the moment I found out I was pregnant. She made me lists of products that I should consider buying or getting second hand. She had even given me a ton of things that she had used for her kids that were still in great condition. I had zero experience with babies, and she had been my personal mommy-concierge. I had even signed up for a lactation class that she had referred me to.

Even Jai couldn't escape Amelia's grasp. She had signed Jai up for New Daddy classes where he would learn how to change diapers and burp babies. I so wished I could have been a fly on the wall in that class just to watch him fiddle with a fake poopy diaper.

"We needed a forklift to bring everything inside," Shyam said, shaking his head.

"It wasn't a forklift! It was a trolley," Amelia corrected, rolling her eyes at her husband.

"You're spoiling my kid, and he hasn't even been born yet," Jai joked.

"I'm the aunty. That's my job," she said defensively.

Jai directed his attention to Dylan. "Hey, bud, what color Lambo do you want?"

The little boy's eyes lit up and his mouth, overstuffed with mashed potatoes, fixed into a huge grin. "Red!" he exclaimed through the mouthful of food.

Amelia shook her head with dread. "Why do I think you're not joking?"

"Because I'm not." Jai's eyes wrinkled as his mouth fixed into a mischievous smile.

My sister-in-law stared him down, giving him the look of death.

"What?! It's my *job* to spoil him," he sang, mocking her words.

"Settle down, children," Shyam commanded the table like he was our father. "Save the carnage for after dinner."

"Yeah, settle down, or Daddy will put you both in time-out," Zayn teased and stuck his tongue out at Shyam.

All I could do was chuckle at their shenanigans.

"So, how was work?" I turned my head to Jai beside me as I tried to settle my laughing fit.

He had made good on his promise and left the drug world behind. Now, he was a married man with an office job and a retirement plan, although he had more than enough money saved up to retire today if he really wanted to.

His position as board member at Sethi Tech kept him fulfilled, especially since he had created the company with his brother.

Shyam had retired as CEO and passed the seat over to Amelia, who had gladly taken the position. Instead, Shyam had settled into another board seat, just like Jai.

Their passion for the company had never died, and now Jai had more time to spend growing the company with his family.

"It was okay. Got into a fight with a board member," he said nonchalantly as he cut into his piece of seasoned chicken.

"With whom?" I gasped. Apparently, his hot temper would never go away, not even in a posh office building.

"Shyam!" Amelia shouted, too impatient to draw out the punchline.

Everyone turned their heads to stare at Shyam in disbelief, waiting for him to deny it. But he never did.

Simultaneously, we all broke into laughter so loud that the baby inside kicked from the ruckus.

"Bet you're wishing you didn't retire as CEO so you could still be Jai's boss, huh?" Zayn asked Shyam as we all tried to catch our breaths.

"Some days I regret it, especially when my *colleague* acts up," he shot back, glaring at Jai. "But my new boss is extra hot." His voice softened as he rubbed Amelia's shoulder. She closed her eyes, savoring his touch.

"Ew, gross." Jai twisted his face in disgust. "That's my boss you're talking about. Have some respect, man!"

Everyone broke out into laughter again. The sound something that happened frequently when we all got together.

I grabbed Jai's hand as the tears of laughter streamed down my face. I felt the smoothness of the wedding band on his finger against my skin. This ring symbolized love and hope, and had replaced his family ring, the one that had caused nothing but heartache and danger for far too long.

Looking around the dinner table, I relished in the happy faces before me, committing them to memory so I could keep them with me forever—my husband and *our* family.

## THE END

*Haven't read about Shyam & Amelia yet and want more of The Sethis? Check out the prologue and first chapter of the bestselling sensation that started it all, Power, right after my Author's Notes & Acknowledgments!*

## Books by Victoria Woods

### The Power Series

#### *Shyam's Duet*

Power

Empowered

#### *Jai's Duet*

Control

Uncontrolled

# Authors Notes & Acknowledgements

It's over. I can't believe it. The Power Series is over after nearly a year since its inception. And I am so incredibly grateful that you stuck around for this journey! Thank you for picking up any or all my books and turning the page for more. I would love if you'd take a moment to leave a review if you enjoyed Uncontrolled. I absolutely adore hearing from you.

When I set out to write Power, I didn't think anyone would want to read it. I had pretty much written it for myself because I felt a void in the romance community. As a woman of color, I had craved novels where other people of color, especially male leads, called the shots.

Eventually I pulled the trigger and decided to create a story about two Indian brothers who were at the tops of their games in the drug world and tech industry. In true mafia style, they were womanizing a\*\*holes, until they met the right women who put them in their respective places. I knew from the moment I started Power that the women wouldn't be Indian and that each brother would be in a multi-racial relationship with a female lead. As far-fetched and unbelievable that mafia romances could be, the truth in my novels would be the relationships between the leads.

Today, we live in a time where relationships are as beautiful and colorful like a rainbow, and I wanted my writing to reflect what I see: people of all races and creeds coming together in the name of love.

So, thank you for coming along on this journey of two Indian guys with big egos, doing illegal things!

There are a few people that I need to thank before signing off for the last time for the Power Series. Without my crew, there would be no Shyam, Jai, or Zayn.

To my ARC readers and street team: How did I get so lucky to have such an awesome team?! You all are my people, and I am so incredibly grateful to each and every one of you. From hustling to read my books in time for release day to promoting material for me, you've gone above and beyond for my works. I love each one of you. Thank you for being my cheerleaders!

To my editor, Paisley: Thank you for showcasing my writing at its best. Time after time, you turn my chicken-scratch manuscripts into pretty lines that magically flow together. You are one no-nonsense woman and I admire you.

To my designer, Cherie: Four covers! I can't believe we've created four covers together. Thank you for all your hard work and last-minute fixes of tiny details that only my neurotic brain would ever care about. You are a saint for putting up with me.

To Daiana: You are a formatting queen! Thank you for making my manuscript beautiful!

To Zoe: You were one of the first people to take a chance on me and my newly released book. Your spirit was such a bright light that it gave me the confidence I needed to promote my work. Ever since then, you've championed me and filled my DMs with excited messages, funny anecdotes, and tons of support. I would have never thought that I'd get to the point where you'd be beta-reading my *fourth* book. Thank you so much for everything!

To Nisha: My PR agent...my beta-reader...my proofreader... my friend. I am so proud of all that you have accomplished in such a short time span. It feels like only yesterday that I was sliding into your DMs to ask you if you would even bother reading my book. I didn't even know how to send ARC copies at the time and failed miserably when I tried to send one to you. Instead, you were patient and took a chance on me. And that chance encounter has turned into a friendship that fills my heart with joy…and now we're releasing books together! You are such a nurturing soul, and I am so lucky to call you "my friend." Ride-or-die, baby! I love you, Soul Sister!

To Amanda: How did this relationship happen?! One minute I'm blindly publishing a book and the next I find my author soul sister who shares the same last name as me! I never thought I'd be lucky enough to be friends with a person who writes with such careful precision as you. Your imagery is unmatched. Every time I read one of your books, I am stunned with the tales that you create. You are my therapist and my ride-or-die. I will always be ready to dig up a begonia bed for you or hop on my horse at a moment's notice. I love you, Soul Sister!

To my husband: Why the hell did you marry me? Seriously? I'm an obsessive control freak who spends all my free time dreaming of plot twists and scandalous things. Instead of giving me side-eye, you encourage me. You always correct me when I say things like "*if* this book takes off…" and remind me to say "*when* this book takes off…" I feel like this writing journey isn't just mine…it's *ours*. I couldn't have asked for a better partner in life. I love you, babe!

Last, but not least, I want to thank you, my reader! You've put your faith in me enough to take my hand and come along on my wild rides and I can't wait to travel amongst the pages again with you.

And with that, "Thank you, Chicago. Goodnight!"

*drops mic and exits stage left as lights dim slowly, bathing the arena in darkness*

# POWER

## THE POWER SERIES: BOOK ONE

## VICTORIA WOODS

# PROLOGUE
## SHYAM

The basement of the warehouse reeked of mold and rusted metal. The stench of blood certainly did not help to quell the foul odor. I kicked the lifeless body splayed out on the discolored concrete floor in front of me. I wanted to make sure the motherfucker was truly dead—as if a bullet to both the head and heart hadn't been enough. We had already stripped away the prosthetics he'd used to disguise his face from us; he now lay naked on the floor like the trash he was.

Traitors like Vik were resilient. Like sewer rats, they always found a way to survive. Some would say that they were good at evasion, but I believed they were just pussies hiding from their imminent death.

A sole set of footsteps echoed from behind me. The sound ceased as another shadow cast over Vik's body, next to mine. My brother and right-hand man, Jai, had arrived. "Is he dead?"

"Where the fuck were you? Busy playing World of Warcraft again?" I asked in reply, my voice dripping with sarcasm. Jai was an IT genius, and he used that genius to run one-half of a tech company that bought up-and-coming startups that created data-tracking software. All these startups provided bits of information that we ultimately used to identify the locations of all other distributors, street sellers, and users. Sethi Tech was a front for our real business...the one that took place in dark alleys, night clubs, and rank warehouses. It kept the IRS and FBI off our backs. That was one of the drawbacks of supplying in the U.S., the fucking government, with all their rules and regulations.

"Fuck you, asshole. I got held up at the office. New acquisition," Jai shot back.

"Yeah, he's dead."

Jai took out his phone and took a picture of the corpse in front of us. I raised my eyebrow in question. "For our records," he said. I knew he had a good reason, so I didn't protest.

Vik had deserved to die. He had been sent by our rival as a spy and had disguised himself as an American street seller, using prosthetics to alter his facial structure so no one would recognize him. He'd paid off a few of our men to approve his background check, so that he could be supplied with product by us, and he had also managed to receive some insider information about our contracts with sellers.

His brother, Tarun, headed our rival organization in India. For years, our organizations had coexisted without any bad blood. It was a convenient situation. I supplied product to most of the United States and Europe, while Tarun's father had supplied his product to the greater part of Asia. Everything had worked smoothly until Tarun's father died and left operations to him. The son of a bitch was greedy and had one hell of a Napoleon complex, so it wasn't long before he broke the rules of peace and sent his bitch of a brother to divert business away from my organization. When my brother heard chatter on the streets about Tarun encroaching on our territory, I started tracking our new salesman using data gathered from various startups we had acquired. We watched his every move for the next month, just to be sure, before taking him out. When Jai analyzed the supply data, he discovered discrepancies. Deep down, I had been holding onto hope it was just rumor and that Tarun was respecting the invisible boundaries both of our organizations had established over the years, because killing Vik would start a war. But Tarun had started this shit, and I would have to end it.

Out of the corner of my eye, I saw a glint of gold below me. Vik's family ring, engraved with a tiger. How fucking cute and stereotypical. A Bengal tiger to represent their headquarters in Bengal. Jai and I had a Sethi family ring, too. Every major supplier family had one. We never took it off. It was another confirmation for me that our new salesman was related to Tarun.

Our ring was made of white gold but had an etched king cobra shaped into an "S," with black diamonds for the eyes. We were the true kings of the underworld, and it was time Tarun realized it.

"Cut the ring off and send it to Tarun's men." They'd relay the message.

# CHAPTER I

## AMELIA

**B**EEP. BEEP. BEEEEEEP.

"Dammit!" I overslept *again* this morning—I had completely missed the first two alarms. If I was late to work, my boss would kill me!

I turned off the third and final alarm, still rattled from being jolted awake, then threw back the covers and ran to my shoe closet of a bathroom to get ready. I could barely move around inside without my legs grazing the toilet or bathtub by accident. The walls were off-white and in desperate need of some fresh paint. I imagined that it was once a bright shade of white, but over time the color had dulled. The grout between the white tiles on the floor was yellow with age and even missing in some spots. Much like the rest of my studio apartment, it was old

311

and cramped. It was outrageous to me that *this* was what two thousand dollars a month could get you in Manhattan, but I didn't really have much of a choice if I wanted to be close to work. The proximity helped whenever I was running late, which seemed to be *always* lately.

I inspected myself in the mirror. The edges were cracked, but I could still see my reflection in the middle of it. God, I was a hot mess! I had stayed up way too late working on code again, and my face showed it. My hair was little more than a tangled auburn nest on my head, and the naturally coarse texture made it difficult to work with on a good day. The bags framing my dark-green eyes nearly matched them in color, and my skin was paler than usual. Even the freckles on my cheeks appeared dull. I really needed to stop working until the sun came up.

Out of time to beat myself up, I quickly brushed my teeth and washed my face. A shower would have to wait until after work. I ran a brush through my hair in an attempt to smooth down some of the frizz, then applied dark brown mascara and nude lip gloss. I threw on a vintage Blondie concert tee over fitted jeans. I took one more look in the mirror, then glanced at the clock and sighed—it would have to do. I stuffed my laptop and headphones into my bag and quickly slipped on my Converse. Then, after locking the door to my tiny apartment, I headed out to face another New York City day.

✳✳✳

"Amelia! Where were you?!" Just as I'd predicted, my boss was pissed. Jason's face was fixed in a scowl as he stood in front of me, arms crossed over his chest. He was a short man with a thin build and thick-framed glasses perched on the bridge of nose. He was in his mid-thirties, yet his hairline was already receding.

"I'm so sorry. I missed my alarms," I said, apologizing earnestly as I slinked into my chair and unloaded my laptop from my bag. I tried to avoid his frigid stare as I powered up my device, praying that it would turn on faster.

"That's the third time this week!" Jason scolded me without any regard for my coworkers overhearing the admonishment. He seemed to be more irritated than usual today, and I sensed it was more than just my tardiness. "I don't have time for this today," he said as he hovered over my desk, then he placed his hands on the tabletop and leaned in, too close for my liking. "I have a meeting right now. We'll discuss this later." Seething with venom, he lingered inches from my face, and I had to stop myself from gagging on the scent of his cheap cologne.

"Your ten o'clock is here," Tammy, his secretary, announced from behind him. Her voice startled Jason, and he snapped up straight and backed away from my desk, but his gaze lingered on me. I exhaled a silent sigh of relief as the space between us grew.

Behind Jason, I saw two tall men standing outside his office. One was dressed in a dark-gray suit, while the other wore a blazer over a black t-shirt and dark jeans. Their strong features

313

shared a resemblance that indicated they were probably related. Both men had darker complexions and black hair, which made them look exotic. They were both handsome at first glance, but the man in the suit had more of an edge to him. His skin was the color of rich honey and he was taller than the other, though only slightly. His angular jaw had a slight shadow of stubble, which contradicted the rest of his polished appearance. His suit was fitted against his lean and muscular body; it was easy to tell he was in shape from how it clung to his tight body. His full lips were pressed tightly together, as if he were clenching his teeth behind them. However, his hazel eyes were the most noticeable aspect of his appearance. They were bright and piercing. I couldn't tear my eyes away from their blaze. They stared back at me with an expression so intense, I was almost scared.

Jason turned around. "Ah, Shyam and Jai Sethi. Thanks for waiting." He extended handshakes to both men and ushered them into his office. Before stepping inside, the taller man glanced at me once more. I squeezed my thighs together under my desk in reflex. Then the door shut behind them, extinguishing the fire that had burned a path to my core.

"Oh. My. God. They're so fucking hot!" Natalie was my desk neighbor and friend who had a keen eye for all things *male*. "I wonder what they're here for," she said as she let out an amorous sigh, leaning back into her desk chair.

Slowly letting out the breath that I had been holding during that heated exchange, I replied, "It seems like something serious, judging from Jason's reaction."

"I bet they're the reason Jason lost his shit on the phone the other day. I heard him shout things like 'takeover' and 'layoff' when I was about to go into his office to get his approval for the new implementation feature," Nat whispered like we were high-school girls gossiping during class.

"Takeover?" I questioned. "You don't think they're here to buy the company?"

The startup was relatively small and new. With about twenty-five employees including Jason, IP Innovations wasn't quite as green as some of the other startups out there, but we were by no means a huge force in the tech world yet. We had made a splash on tech blogs with our facial-recognition software, which could track the locations of people photographed by mobile phones. Facial-recognition software already existed but lacked accuracy for faces of women and people of color. The government had their own version of the software, but ours was the first with a ninety-seven percent accuracy rate. We'd formatted it for social media use, allowing platforms like Facebook and Instagram to recognize faces more inclusively. As a result, it would make "checking-in" easier for users and garner more ratings and reviews for local businesses.

Jason had even been interviewed for *Forbes*'s "30 under 30" list as a result. I guess it was expected that a startup could be bought if they produced successful products, but I hadn't been expecting it to happen to IP Innovations so soon. I had assumed that when the time came, a social media company or even the government would buy our feature and implement it.

IP Innovations had only been up and running for about six months. I liked the other programmers I worked with—minus Jason and his creepiness toward me—and the work itself. I liked it so much that I spent hours coding at home, sometimes well after midnight.

I dreaded being acquired by some enormous tech corporation where we would go from being people with names to just employee numbers. Programmers often lost their passion and drive when these mergers happened, since they were no longer a part of a small, close-knit team.

Nat's voice pulled me from my train of thought. "Well, whatever happens, I wouldn't mind working *under* one of those new bosses…or both!" She licked her lips in the most obscene way, probably playing out some sort of orgy fantasy in her head.

I rolled my eyes. "You have problems!" I redirected my focus back to my laptop monitor and started typing out code.

"No, *you* have problems, missy." She pointed a finger in my face. "You're like asexual! You barely even date. When was the last time you even got laid?" Everything was about sex and how she could get some in Nat's world.

"Hey! I *do* date," I protested. "Last week, I went out with that guy from the advertising company next door, remember?"

"Did you fuck?" she asked, raising an accusatory eyebrow.

"Oh my God, Natalie!" I prayed she would lower her voice before anyone else heard what we were talking about. "I'm not telling you anything," I whispered, hoping she would lower her voice to match mine.

Ignoring my hint, she continued at her regular volume, "That's because there's nothing to tell, or you wouldn't be so uptight right now!"

As much as I hated to admit it, she was right. The advertising guy was cute, but I was so bored at the bar with him that night. He kept talking about himself and barely asked me anything about my life. At one point, I gave up trying to participate in the conversation and instead planned out new coding algorithms that I could use at work in my head. I ended the night early and rushed home to code until four o'clock in the morning.

It wasn't like I was avoiding sex. I was not exactly a virgin, but my experience was fairly limited. I had given a blowjob or two and had some "okay" sex with past boyfriends. I hooked up with a few guys when I first moved to the city, but nothing ever lasted longer than two weeks. I had never experienced anything

317

like the stories Nat would share about her escapades. She was a freak and was into really wild sex. The most adventurous thing I had done was give my high-school boyfriend a blowjob in the backseat of his car after we left the movies one night. To be honest, my orgasms came easier when I was left to my own devices—devices like my vibrator.

I found it difficult to find a guy who could understand my personality. I was an introvert, so putting myself out there and dating was not comfortable for me. The guys I did go out with took advantage of my quietness and overtook our conversations. I didn't think I was socially awkward, but I always doubted myself after dates. Maybe I really was the problem? Maybe I was sabotaging my sexual encounters, and that was why they weren't exciting? Maybe I wasn't capable of being adventurous in bed because I too much of a recluse? I wished I could be more like Nat—assertive and carefree.

Sensing my discomfort, Nat eased up on me. "Come on. Let's take an early lunch and check out that new taco truck down the street. Jason's not even going to know we left," she offered. I was relieved to drop the topic of my sex life—or lack thereof.

*To keep reading more about Shyam and Amelia, check out Power!*

318

# About The Author

Victoria Woods is an International Bestselling Author who enjoys crafting stories filled with suspense, smart female leads, and sexy alpha-males. Inclusion and diversity are important themes in her books. The darker the romance, the better.

A native Floridian, she now lives in Seattle, Washington. Drinking coffee while creating stories as the infamous Seattle rain taps at her window keeps her inspired.

 instagram.com/victoriawoodsauthor/

 goodreads.com/author/show/20896193.Victoria_Woods

twitter.com/VictoriaWWrites

facebook.com/VictoriaWoodsAuthor

Printed in Great Britain
by Amazon